# DEADLIER THAN THE MALE

Skye saw the woman called Apache in the middle of swarming Comanche. Her Colt was blazing. Then rising dust blotted out the scene. Skye heard her bullwhip start to crack. Apache's gun was empty. He rode in to help her.

She was on the ground, fighting off two pony-mounted warriors who were twisting and turning to avoid the whip. Fargo returned his empty Sharps to its saddle case and drew his Arkansas toothpick. Charging the warriors, he stabbed one in the chest, wheeled and slashed the other's arm. The man screamed, then fled.

He dismounted and went to Apache and said, "Are you all right?"

Coiling the bullwhip, she answered, "I'm fine."

The Trailsman had to agree.

# THE
# TRAILSMAN
## 109

# LONE
# STAR
# LIGHTNING

### by

### Jon Sharpe

A SIGNET BOOK

SIGNET
Published by the Penguin Group
Penguin Books USA Inc., 375 Hudson Street,
New York, New York 10014, U.S.A.
Penguin Books Ltd, 27 Wrights Lane,
London W8 5TZ, England
Penguin Books Australia Ltd, Ringwood,
Victoria, Australia
Penguin Books Canada Ltd, 2801 John Street,
Markham, Ontario, Canada L3R 1B4
Penguin Books (N.Z.) Ltd, 182-190 Wairau Road,
Auckland 10, New Zealand

Penguin Books Ltd, Registered Offices:
Harmondsworth, Middlesex, England

First published by Signet, an imprint of New American Library, a
division of Penguin Books USA Inc.

First Printing, January, 1991
10  9  8  7  6  5  4  3  2  1

 REGISTERED TRADEMARK—MARCA REGISTRADA

Printed in the United States of America

PUBLISHER'S NOTE
This is a work of fiction. Names, characters, places, and incidents either are the
product of the author's imagination or are used fictitiously, and any resemblance to
actual persons, living or dead, events, or locales is entirely coincidental.

BOOKS ARE AVAILABLE AT QUANTITY DISCOUNTS WHEN USED TO PROMOTE PRODUCTS OR
SERVICES. FOR INFORMATION PLEASE WRITE TO PREMIUM MARKETING DIVISION, PENGUIN BOOKS
USA INC., 375 HUDSON STREET, NEW YORK, NEW YORK 10014.

# The Trailsman

Beginnings . . . they bend the tree and they mark the man. Skye Fargo was born when he was eighteen. Terror was his midwife, vengeance his first cry. Killing spawned Skye Fargo, ruthless, cold-blooded murder. Out of the acrid smoke of gunpowder still hanging in the air, he rose, cried out a promise never forgotten.

The Trailsman, they began to call him, all across the West: searcher, scout, hunter, the man who could see where others only looked, his skills for hire but not his soul, the man who lived each day to the fullest, yet trailed each tomorrow. Skye Fargo, the Trailsman, the seeker who could take the wildness of a land and the wanting of a woman and make them his own.

*Summer 1860, in west Texas, below Pecos,*
*where outlaws rode in dust devils*
*to plunder, rape, and kill,*
*until one day at sundown . . .*

# 1

The big man astride the magnificent black-and-white Ovaro rode slowly through low-growing greasewood that dominated the flat landscape. Not unlike a black and foreboding sea the individual sun-dried clumps stretched monotonously from horizon to horizon. Stunted mesquite, charred black by the fiery sun, and yucca dotted the dark prairie.

Directly overhead blazed an angry sun as white as the sky in which it hung. It beat down unmercifully on the rider and the sunbaked, desolate terrain.

White alkaline dust covered the man and his horse. Shortly after sunrise he had pulled his neckerchief up to just below his lake-blue eyes. It had done precious little good. The choking dust had quickly plugged his ears and nostrils. A thin layer covered his parched lips, which he refused to lick.

A bone-dry canteen hung from his saddlehorn. He had dripped the last few drops of the tepid water onto the pinto's tongue at sundown the previous day. Earlier he had seen six longhorns foraging for stubbled prairie grass, so he knew water was nearby. An hour passed before he spotted a rather large but shallow depression. He went to it and found the water hole's bottom arid, baked brick-hard. He dug his stiletto between a crack and probed for moisture. Finding none, he mounted up and rode on.

Like the powerful stallion's, the big man's head also drooped. Both sought a measure of relief from the blistering sun. The only sounds came from the tiresome plodding of the horse's hooves. They went unheard by the napping rider.

Dust devils pirouetted among dry Russian thistle, cacti, and the seemingly endless greasewood. A white trail of dust traced their dizzy course.

The prairie and everything on it shimmered in heat waves rising off the scorched and cracked earth. One of the whirlwinds danced out of the rippling waves of heat, uprooted a parched Russian thistle, and tumbled the large ball-like growth into the Ovaro. The stallion snorted a protest at the rough annoyance and deftly hopped his hind legs over it.

Waving the swirling white dust out of his face, Skye Fargo glanced at the dust devil skipping off into the heat waves on his left. Far beyond the playful whirlwind, highly magnified by the ripple effect of the heat waves, loomed a two-story house, barns, and a bunkhouse.

Fargo's first thought was of water. He and the thirsty pinto desperately needed it. He turned toward the ranch house. A lone turkey vulture circling lazily overhead swooped down and lit in front of the house. The meat-eating scavenger's presence meant only one thing: death.

Coming closer, Fargo saw many buzzards huddled on the front steps and at the bunkhouse. The scavengers were stripping rotted flesh off the bones of a man's body lying askew on the steps. The vultures craned to watch Fargo dismount, then, as though unconcerned over having their meal interrupted, hopped onto the porch rail.

Going up the steps, Fargo noted the shotgun lying on the bones of the man's right hand, and the three black crusted bloodstained bullet holes in the front of his shirt. The vultures dropped from their perches and returned immediately to the man's remains when Fargo opened the screen door.

The stench inside the baking-hot room was overpowering. He jerked his neckerchief over his nose. It did little good. He glanced around the room. A narrow staircase led up to the second floor. A woman's body lay on a daybed. Her dress had been ripped in two down the front. It went without saying she'd been sexually violated before the man slashed her throat. The broiling heat had rolled the edges of the wide, deep cut inside out. She hadn't gone down without putting up a fight. Overturned chairs in the otherwise tidy room showed her path of flight.

Fargo stepped into the kitchen. He found her table set for four. The meal was on the stove, cooking when interrupted by the intruder. The food in the scorched pots was unrecognizable. He opened the oven door and saw the blackened remains of a hen that had been baked to a crisp. The hen meant she had been preparing a Sunday supper. He looked at a pailful of drinking water setting on the draining board. Two canteens hung from a peg above the pail. Fargo guzzled from the water bucket. Then he took the canteens and the rest of the water to his horse.

After whetting the Ovaro's thirst, he went back inside and looked up the stairwell. Pulling the neckerchief up over his nose, Fargo took three strides to reach the top landing. Three doors opened as many bedrooms.

He found nobody in the first and presumed it was the man's and his wife's. On the floor in the second room he found the body of a boy that he guessed might have seen his tenth birthday. The youngster's hand still gripped one corner of the sheet he'd pulled from the bed. Flies swarmed over what was left of the lad's face, chewed away from a shotgun blast held close. Fargo shook his head and went to the third door.

A grizzly scene, more hideous than any of the others, greeted him. A girl—by the length of her bloated, nude body Fargo reckoned she was fourteen, certainly not over sixteen—lay with her legs parted wide on the blood-soaked bed. A shotgun blast from close range had blown out her crotch. Fargo hurried outside in an attempt to quell the nausea welling up in his throat. He made it to the porch rail before vomiting. Shaking his head, he watched a buzzard pick in the foul-smelling upchuck.

Fargo cleared his throat and mouth of bile, then ambled to the bunkhouse. He discovered its thatched roof had been burned off, and the length of its interior gutted by the fire. The body of a Mexican man lay sprawled facedown a few feet outside the only door in the bunkhouse. Inside, he found charred remains of six bodies. He presumed they were Mexicans also.

Walking back to the big house he saw a well between it and an adobe barn. He angled for the well. While lowering the water bucket, he looked around the area. Horses and mules stood watching him over the top rail of the corral behind a smaller adobe barn. A chicken coop stood alongside the barn. The chickens inside clucked that they were suffocating-hot. A high board fence was behind the larger adobe structure. Fargo heard pigs grunting behind the fence. Fifty yards left of the house was a rather wide depression. The area between it and the house and barns had been cleared of all growth.

Fargo whistled to the Ovaro. He trotted around the house with his ears perked. After removing the canteens from the saddlehorn, Fargo aimed the pinto toward the depression and slapped his rump. He watched until the thirsty stallion disappeared over the near edge of the ravine, then hauled the bucket of water up.

He drank first, then filled the canteens and poured the rest on top of his head. Temporarily refreshed, he started doing what had to be done.

First he went to the corral and set the horses and mules free. All ran straight to the depression. Then he opened the coop gate and chased the chickens outside. He moved to and looked over the top of the pig's pen. A sow hog and four shoats looked up at him. Their mud hole was bone-dry, baked to a cinder. He let them out. The sow immediately headed for the depression, her squealing brood chasing after her.

Fargo then turned to the sad task of burying the dead. He got a pick and a shovel out of the smaller building and dug two common graves near the well, from which he hauled up water to pour on the hard soil to soften it. Finished, he went to the bunkhouse, where he used partly burned timbers to lay the charred bodies on and dragged them to the grave. After all were in, he shoveled on the soil.

At the house, he used bed linens to drag the family to their grave. He lay the man and wife side by side, then lay the boy on top of his father and the girl atop her mother. He covered them with a sheet, then put the shovel to work.

Finished, he offered a brief prayer, then joined the Ovaro standing knee-deep in the narrow stream that flowed in the depression. Fargo washed his clothes and himself. Draping his gun belt over a shoulder, he took the wet clothing to the house and spread it over the porch rail to dry. Watching the sun go down from where he sat on the front steps, he ate a tin of beans he'd found in the pantry.

He whistled for the Ovaro. When he came to him, Fargo removed the saddle and his other stuff. He put the saddle on the porch rail, his bedroll on the porch, and carried his Sharps and saddlebags upstairs to the front bedroom.

Slipping his Colt under a pillow, he lay on the first bed he'd seen in over a week, and quickly found sleep.

Somebody shouting, "Hey! Anybody home?" jerked his eyes open. His gun hand instantly gripped the Colt. Bright moonlight spilled through the pair of open windows at the side of the bed.

He propped on one elbow and looked down and saw two lean riders. Cocking his Colt, he said, "Yeah. I'm coming down." He strapped the gun belt around his bare waist, holstered the cocked Colt, and went down to see what they wanted.

Standing two paces behind the screen door, Fargo sized up the pair. They appeared young and more like ranch hands than drifters. One wore chaps, both Texas-style cowboy hats. Their hands rested on their pommels, well away from their holstered weapons. Fargo reckoned they were harmless enough, wranglers looking for work.

He stepped onto the porch and asked, "What are you men doing here this time of night? Seems to me you could have waited within sight of the place till morning."

The one on Fargo's left shifted in his saddle and asked amusedly, "Pardon me for asking, mister, but do you always go 'round buck-assed naked at night?"

Clearing his throat, Fargo stepped to the rail and fetched his Levi's. Pulling them on, he answered, "Yes. There isn't anybody around to see me. What brings you way the hell out here?"

The one on Fargo's right answered in high-pitched drawl, "Mister, we're hongry as 'ol Billy Hell. Ain't had a bite to eat in nigh on three days. We couldn't wait for sunup."

Fargo could understand their having hunger pains. He motioned them inside, saying, "Come on in and I'll round up something for you to eat." Inside, he lit a lamp and led the way to the kitchen.

Sitting down at the table, they looked at the four place settings, then glanced questioningly at each other. Fargo saw their curious expressions and explained, "This isn't my place." He went on to say he'd stumbled onto the ranch earlier, found everybody murdered, and spent the rest of the day burying the bodies. Then he asked their names.

High-pitched answered, "Mine's Cooney Roberts."

Chaps said, "And I'm Hank Tyler. You are?"

"Skye Fargo."

"You a cowhand like me and Hank, here?" Cooney asked.

Fargo shook his head and started opening two tins of beans.

Hank asked, "What're you doing in this godforsaken part of Texas, anyhow? Where you headed?"

Fargo felt it best they didn't know he was headed for Austin to keep an appointment. The month-old message penned by State Senator David Winston was handed to him in Tucson by a Butterfield Line Overland Mail celerity stage driver. Winston made it brief:

"Your presence at the state capitol in Austin, Texas, is most urgently requested. You shall receive $500 upon agreeing to accept a dangerous assignment that we will discuss when you arrive." Included in the envelope was $500 to cover Fargo's out-of-pocket expenses to get to Austin. Fargo still had $400 of the advance money tucked in his hip pocket. He answered, "I heard there was railroad work in Texas. Thought I'd look into it."

"I ain't heard about no railroad," Cooney said. "Have you?" He glanced at Hank.

"Nope," Hank offered. "Leastwise not in these parts."

Fargo was ready to move off the railroad subject. Again he inquired why they were here.

Hank finished off his plate of beans before muttering, "Oh, er, uh, hell, Cooney what is the name of that place, anyhow? I forgot."

Cooney leaned back in his chair, sighed, and said, "Shitfire, Hank, I'm getting sick and tired of you saying, 'I forget,' all the time. Now, tell the man where we're going or I'm gonna bust you in the mouth."

Hank stared grim-jawed at Cooney for what seemed an hour to Fargo before scooting his chair back and standing. Leaning over the table, Hank snarled, "Oh, yeah? Who's gonna help you, anyhow, Cooney?"

Cooney hit him square in the mouth. Hank staggered back, shook his head, and dragged the back of his hand across his mouth. He looked at the blood on his hand, then squinted at Cooney. Fargo watched Hank check his teeth and the inside of his lips with his tongue as he balled his hands into fists. Hank was fast. He shot a right jab at Cooney's face and followed it with a left hook just as hard and fast. Cooney was faster. He ducked both fists. Fargo moved back and gave them fighting room.

Hank took a hard blow in his abdomen that doubled him over. Then Cooney wound up and slammed an uppercut into Hank's jaw that straightened him up for the knockout. Cooney gritted his teeth and cocked his right hand to deliver it. Before he could move, Hank spit in his face and swung. Fargo learned Cooney had a glass jaw. It crunched and then Cooney's brown eyes crossed as he dropped to the floor, out cold.

Fargo handed the pail of water to the unsteady victor and asked, "Do you two always settle disputes with your knuckles?"

Hank rinsed out his mouth before answering, "Aw, Cooney's okay. A mite hot-tempered, that's all. Anyhow, I knew if I could get one lick in he'd crumble. Cooney, he can dish it out, but he can't take it. Got anyplace where we can sleep for the night? We'll be gone in the morning." He dumped the pail of water on Cooney's face.

Cooney stirred as Fargo said, "Up the stairs. Put your friend in one bedroom and yourself in the other. They're right across the hall from one another. You might want to flop the girl's bloody mattress."

Fargo watched Hank lift Cooney's limp body and drape it over one shoulder. Tyler smiled, "You want to show the way with the lamp?"

Fargo took him to the girl's room. Hank looked at the blood-soaked bed and said, "Goddamn, that's a whole lot of blood. Where'd you say he shot her, anyhow?"

"In the crotch," Fargo muttered.

Hank dumped Cooney faceup onto the bed. "He won't know the difference till daylight," Hank suggested dryly.

Fargo showed him the boy's room, then left him there and went to his own. He took off his gun belt but not his Levi's. As he returned the Colt to beneath his pillow an uneasy feeling swept through Fargo. He lay down and drifted into sleep realizing neither Hank nor Cooney had said where they were going.

Shortly before dawn his wild-creature hearing alerted him to a soft sound. His eyes snapped open instantly and his gun hand slipped under the pillow. Withdrawing his Colt, he thumbed back its hammer and listened for the sound that had awakened him to come again. It did. One of them was creeping down the hall, coming to his door. The wooden floor squeaking betrayed the intruder.

Fargo sat up, faced the door, aimed at it, and waited. He watched the doorknob turn slowly.

He was applying pressure to the trigger when Hank's voice warned through a window screen behind him, "Shoot that Colt and you're a dead man."

# 2

Hank had climbed up on the porch roof so quietly that Cooney's squeaky footfalls absorbed all sounds outside Fargo's windows. The Trailsman froze and held the pressure on the trigger. He made out the outline of his Sharps leaning against the wall in heavy shadows. The rifle was within easy reach. So was his sheathed Arkansas toothpick, lying on the floor between his feet. But he didn't want to abandon his fast-firing Colt for either of them. Hank was so cocksure he had the drop on Fargo that he had failed to tell him to pitch the Colt on the floor. Fargo tried to keep him from suddenly realizing the mistake by talking.

"What do you want from me, Hank? If it's money, you came to a dry well."

"Shut up," Hank growled. "We'll see for ourselves." In a louder voice he told Cooney, "I have him covered, pardner. Come on in."

It's now or never, Fargo told himself, and fell forward as he fired twice into the door.

Hank's bullet whizzed low over the bed and thudded into the wall beside the door.

Cooney kicked the door open and yelled, "I'll get the big sonsabitch, Hank. Get outta the way."

Fargo heard Hank's footsteps move away from the window. He fired one intimidating shot through the window, swung the Colt around, and fired another through the doorway. Grabbing his rifle, he dived through the window. Glass flew in all directions as the dry wood in the window splintered and gave way under the heavy impact. The screen broke free. Fargo tumbled off the roof. Hank fired at the moving target and missed. Fargo landed on his feet.

He backed out into the front yard several paces and saw Hank's shadowy form go through the shattered window. He shot anew, anyhow, and dashed for the front door. Yanking it open, he yelled, "I'm coming up to get you two yellow-bellied, sneak-thief cowards." Crossing to the stairs, he tracked their footsteps on the bedroom floor above. He heard one pair get into firing position to greet him on the stairs. The other pair moved across the bedroom, then across the porch roof. Fargo heard a dull thud when the man's feet hit the ground.

Hank yelled, "I'm on the ground, Cooney. We have him now. He's got one bullet left."

What fools, Fargo thought. Men acting like children. He decided to end their fleeing through the greasewood. Going up the stairs, Fargo emptied the Colt, then fired the Sharps once. He heard Cooney holler, "Aw, shit," then his bootsteps running to the window.

By the time Fargo made it back to the porch, they were riding away in a dead run, leaning on their horses' necks. He retrieved the rest of his clothing and sat on the front steps to dress as he watched dawn break.

Back in the saddle, he watched the sun rise. A thin red arc at first, then the huge, fiery orb seemed to explode over the horizon. Soon the heat waves appeared, then dust devils sprang to life and swirled from south to north. A rattlesnake as big around as Fargo's wrist and much longer than his arm slithered out of the Ovaro's path. Fargo watched the rattler coil and start its buttons to buzzing. He looked for its prey. A cactus mouse stood within striking distance. It squeaked as the reptile struck and sunk its deadly fangs into the little creature's body. A roadrunner darted among clumps of greasewood in front of the pinto, paused, then sped away. Fargo pulled his neckerchief up below his eyes, lowered his head, and rode into the rising sun.

At sundown he reined the stallion to a halt between

two scrubby, dead mesquite and made camp. The Ovaro was relieved of his burden and set to graze on patches of prairie grass. Then Fargo broke off mesquite limbs and made a small cooking fire to brew a pot of coffee. Soon the aroma of coffee wafted among the mesquite, greasewood, and prickly pear. A rapid drop in temperature came as night fell. Fargo sat close to the fire.

Sipping coffee from his tin cup, Fargo thought of the ranch family. It wasn't enough for the man, or men, to violate the rancher's wife and daughter. No, they'd also been murdered, and in a most vicious way. "Clearly, the butcher is deranged," he mused aloud to the fire. Fargo thought about the man's motive. It was obvious the murderer was well-fed. He hadn't partaken of the food. So hunger wasn't the motive. Jealousy? About what? he wondered. The only thing Fargo could imagine was success. And that implied that a neighboring rancher had committed the heinous crime. Encroachment? No, there was plenty of land to go around. Drifters? Maybe. But drifters are always hungry.

No, the rancher had known the culprit. And had been wary of him. He'd brought his shotgun with him when he stepped out onto the porch. That suggested they'd had dialogue before the man shot him to death.

About what? Fargo asked himself. The shots would bring the ranch hands running from the bunkhouse. And that meant there were several deadly men involved in the massacre. Fargo ruled out Apaches and Comanches. They would have taken the women captive and scalped the males. He also ruled out Hank and Cooney, for the simple reason that they would have remained in the house and taken liberties with the females at their leisure after killing the ranch hands and rancher. Besides, there was the matter of the uneaten food. The more Fargo thought about it, the more he concluded it was the work of an organized gang of outlaws. And that brought him back to the question of motive. One thing was for sure: they weren't rustlers.

Fargo quit thinking about it because he knew he'd never learn the cause of what had happened. He downed the last of the coffee, then spread his bedroll and snuggled inside it. The stars were extra brilliant. Drifting into sleep, he looked at constellations long familiar to him. Like beacons to seamen crossing the oceans, they also guided the Trailsman overland at night.

His internal clock wakened him shortly before dawn. Relieving himself, he looked at the morning star. Other stars were already twinkling out, but the morning star would be the last to fade. After saddling the Ovaro, he rolled up his bedding and secured it behind the saddle. Then he mounted up and rode toward the morning star, fading rapidly in dawn's early light. Shortly, the red rim of the sun peeked over the horizon to herald yet another murderously hot day.

At sunset, after a long day's ride, he rode into an adobe village that straddled the banks of a dry riverbed.

Muted, mournful guitar music being strummed softly came from somewhere in the village. The haunting melody sent a chill down Fargo's spine.

Mexican youngsters paused in their play to watch the big Anglo riding toward them. Mothers darted out of the hovels that lined the narrow dirt corridor, grabbed up their young, then fled back inside. The other children backed against the adobe walls to allow the Ovaro passage. As though he were the devil himself, they stared fearfully at Fargo. He shot them a wink.

Coming out of the tight passageway, he passed a young priest stringing twine, laying the lines for a mission that fronted one side of the small village square. Several Mexican women were queued around the community well in the center of the square, drawing water to fill their *ollas*. Fargo and the priest exchanged nods.

The guitar music grew louder. It came from somewhere down the narrow street across the parched riverbed. Fargo rode toward the music and found it came from within the village *cantina*. He dismounted and went inside. A candle sat on the short bar. Its flame provided the only light in the compact room. About a dozen Mexican men sat at tables facing the guitarist. Bottles of warm *cerveza* and tequila sat on the table-tops. Nobody drank from them. At first, while his eyes adjusted to the heavily shadowed interior, Fargo missed seeing the guitarist. The young man sat on the hard-packed earthen floor with his back to the rear wall, absorbed in darkness much like the melody he played. The fat bartender stood behind the bar, resting his weight on his elbows by the candle. His dark eyes and perspiring plump face shone brightly in the candlelight.

When Fargo stepped to the other side of the candle, he broke the bartender's fixation on the guitar player. The man glanced up, then started to tremble. The fellow's expression conveyed stark terror as he backed against the wall. The guitarist instantly ceased strumming. The patrons momentarily faced Fargo, then hurried outside.

"Bourbon, if you have it," Fargo said.

The bartender edged along the wall, eyeing the front door nervously.

Fargo asked in Spanish, "Are you deaf? I asked for bourbon."

The fat man gulped, "No, *señor.* I have *cerveza* and tequila. Nothing else."

"Then I'll take a bottle of tequila. How much is it?" He dug a handful of coins out of his front pocket.

The bartender started waving his hands and shaking his head. "It's free, *señor* . . . to you." He brought a bottle of tequila from a shelf below the bartop and handed it to Fargo.

Fargo dropped a four-bit piece on the bar. Pulling the cork, he asked, "You act afraid of me. Why?"

The guitarist answered, "Héctor fears you are one of the Anglo desperadoes come to kill him."

Fargo faced the guitar player. When he did, Héctor ran outside. Fargo swilled from the bottle, then asked, "Anglo desperadoes?" Hank and Cooney crossed his mind.

*"Sí, señor."*

Fargo watched the lean young man rise, lay his

guitar on top of a table, and come behind the bar. He reached under it and got a bottle of *cerveza*. As he opened it, their eyes met. "My name is Manuel, *señor*. The Anglo gang comes to Río Pecos all the time." Manuel kept his eyes on Fargo's when swigging from the bottle.

"Why? To drink and raise hell?" Fargo couldn't imagine Hank and Cooney leading a gang of men—or riding with one, for that matter. "How many men are there in this gang?" Fargo asked.

"Six men, *señor* . . . and one woman. They make us pay money to protect us. Don Diego, too. They kill a few of our men, rape a few of our *señoritas* every time they come to our little village. That's what you heard me playing about 'Río Pecos Is Slowly Dying.' Some of the people have gone back to Mexico. It's very bad here, *señor*."

"Don't you people have guns?"

Manuel shook his head. "No, *señor*. Don Diego won't allow us to have guns."

"Oh? Who, what is this Don Diego who has so much power over your lives?"

Manuel took a long pull from the bottle of beer before answering, "Don Diego was here first. He brought us to tend his cattle and till the soil. Don Diego's *hacienda* is far downstream. We rarely see him."

Fargo felt saddened over the plight of the defenseless peons. He decided to pay Don Diego a visit tomorrow to try to talk some sense into the man's hard head. That was the least Fargo could do. Surely the delay in keeping his appointment in Austin would be understood by David Winston. But Fargo didn't say any of that. Instead, he asked, "Where is the corral and a place to bathe?"

"We are farmers, *señor*. There is no corral here. The corral is at the *rancho*. We have only a pen for our goats and burros. The shed is at the end of the street. Follow your nose. We have two places to bathe: one for the women, one for the men. Both are in arbors at opposite ends of the village. The men's is across the river." Manuel went on to give Fargo directions.

Nodding, Fargo took the half-empty bottle outside. Easing up into the saddle, he heard Manuel start strumming "Rio Pecos Is Slowly Dying."

Fargo rode to the pen and put the pinto inside. After removing his bedroll and saddle, he gave the horse a bucket of water to drink.

Sensing somebody was watching him, he spun around and brought his Colt from its holster, up and ready to fire. A young woman flattened her back to the wall across the narrow street. She gasped, "Don't shoot me, *señor*."

Fargo uncocked the hammer and holstered the gun. Stepping to the fence rails, he said, "Girl, don't ever sneak up on me again. The next time I may shoot first and ask questions later. Now, who are you and what do you want?"

She visibly relaxed. She moved toward him and he saw that her shapeliness was marred only by a rather wide fanny. She held a chunk of soap and a wash rag. Standing in front of him with her hands behind her back, she looked up at him and said, *"Mi nombre es Lucita, señor. ¿Cómo se llama?"*

"Skye Fargo."

"Manuel said you wanted to take a bath. He told me you were at the goat pen. There is a water hole down the river, a short walk's distance. Or do you want to bathe in the arbor? I can't scrub your back in the arbor."

He looked into her pleading eyes and saw a terrible lustful yearning. "The water hole will be fine." He handed her the bottle, then fetched his bedroll, Sharps, and draped the saddlebags over one shoulder. "Lead the way," he suggested.

Going to the water hole, Lucita swigged from the bottle. They chatted between her slugs of tequila. "Like the others, aren't you afraid of me, Lucita?"

"No," she replied. "I watched you ride in alone. I knew you weren't bad like the other Anglos who come to hurt us."

24

"Have they ever hurt you?"

"The one named Clarence does. He gets drunk and beats me. Clarence always says the same thing: 'Lucita, get down on them hands and knees. I'm gonna split that big ass of yours wide open.' He never does, though. Too small. I don't ever feel it. But I act like he's tearing me up. I scream and yell for him to quit. That way he won't shoot me afterward."

Fargo was more interested in the woman gang member. "What does the female with them do while all this is going on?"

"Bad Addie? She sits at a table in the cantina and drinks *cerveza* while collecting everybody's money. She shoots those who don't have any. Héctor drags the bodies out in the street and puts them on a cart."

Fargo described Hank and Cooney. Lucita shook her head, saying, "I've never seen them." Pinching her left cheek, she added, "I'm feeling this tequila," and raised the bottle to her lips.

After that they walked in silence until they arrived at the water hole. It was larger than Fargo had imagined, and much clearer. The moon's image reflected off the still surface. Fargo dropped the bedroll and saddlebags between two patches of green greasewood.

As he spread the bedroll, Lucita shimmied her loose-fitting flimsy cotton sundress down her body and stepped out of it. Kneeling, she undid the buttons on his fly, reached in, and withdrew his member. Glancing up at him, she whispered, "Nice. May I taste it?" Lucita proceeded to do just that.

Fargo dropped his Sharps onto the saddlebags, entwined both hands in her long black hair, and coaxed her to take in more than the head. She "uhmed" and "ahed" down his length, then slowly inched her way up. Her tight lips smacked when they left his summit.

She sighed, "I can't wait to get it in me. Are you going to do me like Clarence does?"

Fargo ran and dived into the moon's reflection, Lucita right behind with the soap and rag. He swam underwater to the far side and back, then sat with his back to her in the shallow part. After scrubbing his back and broad shoulders, she reached around his neck and began washing his chest. He felt her nipples teasing back and forth, up and down as she rubbed first his left pectoral muscle, then the right.

Feeling his right biceps, she murmured, "My, but you have a *muy bonito cuerpo*, big man. So powerful, so strong. Your muscles are hard like rocks." Lucita lowered a hand to his organ and squeezed it, mewing childlike, "And this one is hardest of all. So nice, so big."

Fargo pulled her over his left shoulder. She squealed and giggled, delighted that he would play with her. He dunked her several times. Each time she came up gulping for air. Finally, he embraced her and they kissed openmouthed. The kiss was all it took to end their play. Lucita's breathing quickened. She straddled his lap, rubbed her full breast over his chest, rose on her knees, and took his face in her hands and circled his lips with her hot tongue. His crown parted her lower lips. He grasped her broad hips. She squatted, he thrust.

Shoving down harder, she moaned, "Oh, oh, that feels so good. Oh, yes, it feels good."

Fargo set her hips to swaying. She paused to make his manhood glide in and out, rub on the top of the tender opening. Her hand curled around his neck, and her head lolled as she whimpered, "Give all of it to me, please, please . . . Oh, yes, that's it, that's it. You're driving me *loca*." Through clenched teeth, Lucita screamed, "Aaagh! Aaah! Faster, faster!"

Fargo sucked in all of her left breast his mouth could hold and teased the nipple and swirled the areola. She gasped, "Oh . . . oh . . . yes, yes . . . don't stop . . . please, don't," and screamed, "I'm coming, I'm coming!"

He felt the contractions seize around him and start milking his full length, which was in deep. He couldn't hold back any longer. The eruption came in spurts, and she gasped, "Good . . . good . . . fill my belly. Oh, God, yes . . . so wonderful."

They clung to each other, she kissing his face and

ears, neck and shoulders, he nibbling her nipples and breasts, until he limbered. He cradled her in his arms, carried her to his bedroll, and lowered her onto it.

She pulled him atop her wet body, looked into his eyes, and whispered, "You're wonderful. You've made me feel like a woman again, not a pig like Clarence does."

Fargo touched a finger to her lips to hush her. Tears of happiness welled in the young peasant woman's eyes, then burst forth and trickled down her cheeks. He kissed her, then they slept under the moon and stars.

The sun beating down on Fargo awakened him. Lucita's head nestled in the crook of his left shoulder, her sleeping face a study in pleasure. He fondled a breast to awaken her. She stirred as her eyes fluttered open. She smiled sleepily and mumbled, " 'Morning. Are we in heaven?"

He chuckled. "We are if cactus and greasewood grow there. We have to hike to find a breakfast which you are going to fix." He touched her nose to emphasize the comment.

Lucita stretched sensuously, yawned, and got up. Fargo watched her dive into the water, swim several strokes, then come out. He walked in and splashed water on his face, neck, and shoulders, then they dressed. She carried his saddlebags and Sharps back to the village.

A dozen clucking chickens greeted them. At the goat pen, he put his bedroll and saddlebags on top of his saddle. Lucita hugged an arm around his waist and took him to her home to feed him.

An older woman and six children were there. A precocious girl, no older than four, looked into Fargo's eyes and smiled winsomely. He shot her a wink and returned her engaging smile. The woman glared at Fargo, then stared at Lucita. No words were needed to convey the woman's shame; her eyes said it all. Quietly but quickly she ushered the youngsters outside and followed the last one through the doorway.

"My sister thinks I'm *muy mala*," Lucita explained.

"I'm not. Is it a sin to give and receive happiness?" She cracked six eggs into a skillet, cut up two green chiles, and scrambled the whole lot.

Fargo sat at the table to watch and listen to her talk to herself. "I want out of Río Pecos, out of Don Diego's bean fields, out of all their misery." Pointing a wooden spoon at him, she went on, "They'll kill all of us before it's over. Clarence will shoot me where he shot poor Esmeralda Gómez. I told her to scream, but she wouldn't listen. Esmeralda told me she'd grit her teeth before she would scream and give Clarence the pleasure of believing he had hurt her with his little thing."

The rancher's daughter flashed in Fargo's mind's eye. "What do you mean by 'where he shot her'?" He was sure of the answer before it came, but he wanted it verified.

Setting the skillet of scrambled eggs and a dish of leftover tortillas on the table, Lucita answered, "Clarence shoved his sawed-off, double-barreled shotgun up her butt and pulled both triggers. He laughed like a madman. The tortillas are cold. Want me to warm them?"

Fargo shook his head. "Do any of the others use a knife to kill?"

"The one called Wichita does. He cut Lupita's throat wide open after saying she didn't move her ass fast enough for him. Buddy has a knife, too. A big one with a deer foot for a handle. Sure you don't want me to warm up the tortillas?"

Fargo folded a tortilla over a helping of the eggs and chiles and munched his way down the arrangement. He suspected the gang—what did Lucita call the female? Bad Addie?—had killed the rancher, his family, and everyone else for failure to pay up. Like Lucita predicted, and Manuel's foreboding melody promised, the gang would end up killing every soul in Río Pecos, too. Fargo finished his breakfast and pushed back from the table. It was high time he met Don Diego.

He told Lucita, "I'd advise you people to start walking back to Mexico. Loyalty to this Don Diego is one thing, but the virtue, under the prevailing circumstances, is slowly and surely killing you. Get out of Río Pecos while you still can. Leave today."

Lucita stared at him as though a bright light had appeared at the far end of a long dark tunnel, as though what he'd said suddenly made sense. She nodded. She walked him to the pen and watched him make the Ovaro ready for the trail.

Before mounting up, he hugged and kissed her.

She stood at the end of the corridor, surrounded by children, and watched him disappear in the heat waves, never realizing the urgency of his advice.

# 3

Following the river downstream, Fargo watched thunderheads build in the southwest. The heat waves still undulated and dust devils cut their erratic courses among the greasewood, but the calm air held a hint of moisture.

In midafternoon Fargo found a stretch in the river where water stood. He dismounted to drink from it and water the Ovaro. A light breeze rippled the surface, brushed his face. He glanced at the black clouds moving toward him. Silent lightning flashed in them. As though by magic, the heat waves and then the dust devils vanished. Fargo returned to his saddle and rode onward, into the face of the summer storm.

Soon wind howled over the parched, flat land. Black roiling clouds, low to the ground, blotted out the burning sun. The sky became eerily dark. He watched a gray curtain drop from the churning clouds. Behind the gray wall the clouds turned ghostly green. Sheets of wind-driven rain blasted into Fargo and the stallion, instantly transforming the baked earth into a muddy sea. Rainwater cascaded over the banks of the river, quickly filling it, making it surge angrily downstream. Then came dime-sized hail. Fargo watched it bounce off the mud and cover the ground, much like a frozen tundra. The Ovaro wanted to put his tail to the wind, rain, and hail. Fargo let him.

The pungent smell of creosote permeated the air. Bolts of lightning stabbed down and exploded. Thunder boomed. Through it Fargo heard a locomotive roaring. Glancing behind, he saw the twister's ugly snout dip from the angry clouds and touch the ground.

Greasewood, cacti, and mesquite, anything and everything in the funnel's path, were sucked up into it, then spit out. Fargo was in its path.

He reined left and put the mighty stallion into a dead run to escape the onrushing twister. Its furiously revolving funnel plunged into the rain-swollen river, sucked up the muddy water, and hurled it in all directions. Fargo slowed the Ovaro's gait to a lope. He turned and watched the twister move upstream, leaving the debris of the prairie in its wake.

When he looked ahead, the vague shape of a large structure loomed through the downpour. Coming closer, he came to two stone columns supporting a wrought-iron arch. Pausing under the arch, he read lettering on it that spelled RANCHO DE SUEÑO. A hundred yards in front of him glowed several pale-yellow rectangles of light in the large structure and a row of them in the low structure he now saw left of it.

As he approached the ranch house, lightning flashed and showed Fargo the exterior of one of the grandest mansions he'd ever seen. Red Spanish tile covered the roof of the two-story stucco structure. Eight gleaming, white marble columns supported the second-level balcony. Lamps burned in all the front rooms. The wide, deep porch behind the marble columns was constructed of reddish-brown Mexican tile a foot square. So were the ten wide steps leading up to it. Fargo didn't hesitate as he rode up the steps.

The wind and rain lashed him as he sat in the saddle and pounded on the twin massive oak doors. Twin windows, the height of the door, framed them. The lamp in the room on his left was snuffed out. Then those on his right. Fargo continued to pound on the doors.

After a long moment one opened by a hand's width. A boy about the age of twelve peered out. The lad's eyes were filled with fright and he trembled uncontrollably.

Fargo pushed both doors wide open and rode inside. The boy hurried to close the doors, to stop the rain following the big stranger. Lightning flashed and the brilliance momentarily spilled through the twin windows and lit up the space, which Fargo saw was the foyer, and a spacious one at that. A blood-red carpet covered the wide staircase leading to the upper level. Closed sliding doors connected rooms on both sides of the cathedral-ceiling foyer. A grandfather clock stood against one wall. And Fargo noticed the boy had moved to the door on his left and flattened his back and outstretched arms across it defensively.

Fargo dismounted and said, in Spanish, "I'm here to see Don Diego. What's your name?"

Gulping down fear, the boy stammered, "Ju-Ju-lio. Señor Rodríguez and his, his family are away . . . on business, in, uh, yes, Mexico City." The boy's right hand moved to the door's ivory handle.

"Well, then, Julio, they won't mind me staying here till they return, will they?"

Julio's widened eyes darted nervously left and right. Fargo was in a quandary over what to do with him and the stallion dripping water on Don Diego's tiled floor. When he stepped to the door, Julio grabbed its handle and gasped, "No, *señor*! I beg you—"

Fargo pulled him aside and slid the door open. He waited for lightning to flash in the storm raging outside. Seeing the lamp, he crossed the room and lit it. Julio watched Fargo's every move from just inside the doorway. Fargo scanned the stately room, appointed lavishly with rich blood-red leather wingbacks and a matching couch arrangement that faced a huge fireplace. Heavy oak tables stood below the massive black oak rafters that lined in the stucco ceiling. A liquor cabinet stood against one wall. The large oil painting hanging above the fireplace mantel portrayed a short, paunchy fellow in his fifties, who would surely prove to be the ranch's owner. The painting dominated the room.

Fargo pointed to it and asked, "Don Diego?"

Julio hesitated briefly, then nodded and asked, "*Señor*, do you want Carlota to prepare a meal for you . . . before you go?"

"Coffee will do. And please have my horse stabled and fed."

After calling for another servant to tend the horse, the boy led Fargo through the dining room. A ten-foot-long dining table—heavy oak, of course—that seated eight had place settings for three. Two silver candelabra, spaced apart evenly, stood on the table. The six candles in them were lit.

They entered a spacious kitchen. A middle-aged, plump woman sat by the table shelling peas. Julio called her by name and said Fargo wanted coffee.

Carlota smiled graciously and nodded when she rose and got a cup off a shelf. Fargo knew he had interrupted the evening meal Carlota was preparing. The aromas of roast chicken and pork seeped from the oven and mixed with pots of vegetables on top of the stove. Carlota poured him a cup of the brew and handed it to him. He checked inside the pantry while sipping from it.

"Where are they?" Fargo asked.

Carlota glanced at the boy, who answered, "Monterrey."

"Before, you said Mexico City," Fargo reminded dryly.

Julio shrugged.

As he went through the mansion, Fargo lit every lamp he found. He searched each room and closet, every nook and cranny without finding any evidence that the Rodríguezes were there. When he stopped to listen for a telltale sound, the boy waited in silence at a discreet distance. Fargo returned to the room adjacent to the foyer and crossed to the liquor cabinet. He said, "I want a word with Don Diego about leaving his laborers in the village defenseless, at the mercy of the gang of desperadoes." He found no bourbon. He selected whiskey instead.

When he turned, he saw the man in the painting had manifested. Rodríguez, flanked by two women, one older and much stouter than the frail one on his left, stood in the doorway, gaping at the stallion.

Fargo muttered amusedly, "Fast trip. A dry one, too, I see."

Don Diego looked at him questioningly.

Fargo swigged from the bottle before saying, "I'm Skye Fargo, not a desperado. Some people call me the Trailsman. The ladies names are . . . ?"

The fellow hurried across the room to the liquor cabinet. Fargo noticed he didn't bother to make a selection, just grabbed the first bottle he touched. Shaking hands raised the bottle of gin to his mouth and he gulped it half-empty. Julio and the two women watched Diego drag the back of his hand across trembling lips. He looked at Fargo and in a cracking voice asked, "Why are you here? What do you want of us?"

Nodding toward the women, Fargo repeated, "Who are they?"

Diego answered, "My wife, Teresa, and my daughter, María."

At that moment, the grandfather clock started chiming. The tolling ended after striking eight times.

Concurrent with the last peal, Carlota appeared behind Teresa and María and announced the evening meal. The women turned and immediately followed her. Julio and the two men tarried a moment longer. Fargo told Don Diego he had just arrived in Río Pecos, that he wanted to talk to him about the sorry conditions he found in the village, but it could wait until the meal was finished.

Gesturing for Fargo to precede him to the dining room, Diego said, "I am Don Diego Rodríguez y Hernández, at your service, *señor*."

He found the women already seated at the table, the mother at one end and the daughter at its middle, across from a fourth place setting that Fargo knew was his.

Carlota had spread a feast. The baked hen, plump and juicy, set between Fargo and María, the roast beef within easy reach of Don Diego, and the pork roast near Teresa. Each platter was flanked by cooked and raw vegetables. Baskets of fruit lay among the bowls of vegetables and platters of meat. A bottle of fine French red wine stood in front of each place setting. A bowl of tossed salad was waiting next to his napkin when Fargo sat.

He filled his wineglass and studied María over its rim while sniffing its bouquet. A flat-chested woman with black hair done up in a bun, she had large eyes set rather wide apart, surrounded by weak coffee-colored hues. The soft-brown tones made her appear both sad and sensuous. Fargo wondered which appearance dominated. When she tipped her glass to sip from it, she looked at Fargo. He saw desire in her dark eyes.

Diego clearing his throat broke their eye contact. Fargo shifted his gaze to him as Rodríguez asked, "What conditions?"

Fargo worked off about half his salad before answering, "The peasants have no weapons."

"*Sí, sí,* I know that," Don Diego barked. "No weapons are allowed on my ranch."

"Why?" Fargo probed.

Teresa motioned Carlota to bring the soup and answered, "Because, *señor*, they would only get drunk and shoot one another." Teresa looked down the length of the table at her husband for his verification of the statement.

Fargo thought it a mighty strange philosophy. He perceived the true answer was that Don Diego refused to arm them for fear they would turn against him.

Shrugging, Diego added to his wife's comment, "The Anglo *bandidos* kill fewer of them than they would if I gave the peasants guns to shoot back. Believe me, *señor*, when I say, then you would see the *bandidos* carry out a real slaughter." He dipped a soup spoon into his bowl.

The remainder of the sumptuous meal was eaten in silence. María continued to eye Fargo. She shot him a provocative smile once that promised much. He reckoned the young woman was desperate for a man, being confined in the mansion and refusing to lower her status by romping with a lively ranch hand in the haystack. She started sucking grapes from a cluster, watching Fargo all the while. Juice covered her lips and ran down her chin.

Finally, Fargo spoke. "I need a bath and a place to sleep for the night. I'll be leaving at dawn or whenever the storm passes, which ever comes first."

Diego's heretofore somber spirits instantly perked up. So did the *señora*'s, but not the *señorita*'s. Panic flashed across the girl's ashen face. Visibly stiffening, she stared across the table at Fargo. He saw urgency in her pleading eyes.

Teresa said, "A maid will prepare your bath, *señor*."

Diego suggested he and Fargo return to the parlor to drink and smoke cigars while waiting.

Pushing back from the table, Fargo shot María a wink. She relaxed and smiled happily.

In the parlor, Diego poured bourbon for Fargo and Scotch for himself. Then he opened a half-empty box of small cigars and removed two, saying proudly, "I have them rolled especially for me in Cuba."

Fargo sniffed the skinny cigar before wetting it. He lifted the lamp's flue and lit the cheroot, then moved to the couch and sat. Diego stepped to the fireplace and struck an identical pose to the one in the painting.

Pompous little bastard, Fargo thought, but said, "I want you to know I have advised everybody to leave Río Pecos."

"What?" gasped Diego. The revelation set him to pacing. "Why?" he shouted, red in the face.

Fargo reckoned that the angry man was ready to burst a blood vessel. Don Diego broke his cigar in two and threw the pieces into the fireplace.

Fargo spoke evenly. "You heard me. That gang of butchers is methodically killing them. How long has it been going on?" He watched the older man run a hand over his graying hair.

Don Diego stopped pacing and faced him. "Six, seven months. What difference does it make, you meddling cowboy?"

With a controlled menace in his voice that was more

frightening than violent, Fargo quietly said, "The difference, you blithering idiot, is you're standing by while good men and women and, yes, little children are being murdered. Have you no compassion for your countrymen? And, I'm not a cowboy!" He continued, keeping his anger on a tight leash, "It's high time you prayed for the souls you and that sanctimonious wife of yours have murdered in the name of 'no self-defense is the best defense.' Don Diego, I despise you."

Shaking like a quaking aspen leaf, Diego hurriedly crossed himself and started mumbling what sounded like a prayer.

Fargo left him in that position and went in search of his bath. María met him at the top of the staircase and led him to a tub of hot water in the bath area adjoining his bedroom. When she slipped off one shoulder strap of the flimsy sheath she had changed into, Fargo snapped testily, "Thank you, but you're no longer needed."

Rebuked, she fled, crying.

Fargo undressed and immersed himself in the hot water. All of his pent-up tension faded away as he lay back and relaxed. The maid, a petite young woman, appeared in the doorway with an armful of towels. She begged his pardon and claimed she had overlooked putting out towels for him. Fargo nodded the oversight. She draped the towels on a rack, then quickly left. Fargo knew she was burning up with curiosity to see the big Anglo stranger who brought the aristocrats to their knees and forced them to humble themselves before God. Julio had told her. Fargo had seen him standing in the shadows of the foyer, watching and hearing everything. Fargo hoped the boy would spread the word like a raging wildfire.

He soaked while listening to thunder rattle the rain-drenched windows next to the tub, until the water cooled. He slipped under the covers of the canopied, four-poster bed made from heavy oak, leaned over, and blew out the lamp. Rain beat on his window. When lightning flashed and lit up the room, he saw book cases filled with books on both walls next to the only door in the bedroom. A small fireplace occupied the wall opposite the large window. He drifted into sleep listening to the raindrops' tattoo on the window-panes.

Much later, his eyes snapped open. His right hand slipped beneath his pillow, gripped and cocked his Colt. He looked at the window. Dawn was starting to break. The wind and rain had ceased. The storm had passed. But that wasn't what had caused him to awaken. Then his nostrils caught a whiff of a delicate perfume. He turned his head to face the fireplace.

María stood there, naked as at the moment of her birth. Large nipples protruded from tiny areolae on her flat chest. Her rib cage showed, and so did her hipbones and collarbones. But she had one of the bushiest, blackest patches of pubic hair Fargo had ever seen. He raised his gaze to her eyes and saw that she was unsure of what he would do. He wondered how she had opened the door without his hearing it. Gently lowering the hammer of his Colt, he beckoned her to approach.

She whispered, "I lay awake all night, wondering if you were still angry with me."

"How did you get in here?" He drew back the covers and gestured for her to enter the bed.

María eagerly slipped between them and snuggled her slim body against him. She didn't answer his question, whispering instead, "Oh, how I've longed for a man such as you to come along and bed me. My groin aches to be satisfied. Oh, how I ache."

He slid a hand over her nipples. When he did, she trembled and moaned. He lowered his hand to her quivering belly, then dipped it into the sable patch and touched her hot, moist opening. She clamped her thighs to capture the finger rubbing her slit. Fargo probed with his finger. She gasped, "Oh . . . oh."

He rolled atop her. Her knees came up and she positioned the head for penetration. Before he could thrust, somebody started pounding on the front door. A man's voice shouted in a southern drawl, "All right, Dee-a-go, open up or I'll kick the fucking door in."

María stiffened, tight as a banjo string. She forgot all about sex, pushed Fargo off her body, and bolted upright in the bed.

Fargo grabbed his Colt and headed for the door.

She left the bed, ran, and grabbed his arm. Terrified, she said, "No! Don't go. It's Leonard and his band of thieves. Please, there are too many of them for only one man. Father will pay them money, then they will leave. You'll see." María started pulling him toward the bookcases.

"What are you doing?" he asked, confused. "Where?"

María pulled on a bookcase. It swung out noiselessly. She stepped into the wall space it had hidden, and motioned for him to follow her. Fargo stepped into the tight space. He had to turn sideways to keep his shoulders from scraping on the walls. María closed the opening. They stood in pitch-black darkness. He felt her cold hand find his.

Gripping it, she whispered, "I'll lead you down to the parlor. Watch your footing."

He felt his way through the darkness and down stone steps. She stopped. Twin rays of lamplight suddenly stabbed through two minuscule holes in the wall. María put her eyes to them. Fargo heard the same man's callous voice order, "Hurry up, you greasy piece of shit. And don't give me any backtalk."

Don Diego spoke in a whiney, trembly voice, "I'm hurrying. I'm hurrying."

Fargo nudged María out of the way and put his eyes to the holes. He saw Leonard, two other men, and the female. Leonard was a big, rough-looking man. A short black beard and mustache framed his biscuit-dough face. Cruel, penetrating eyes watched Diego from sunken sockets. Low-riding holsters held two Smith & Wesson army issues. He wore no hat.

One of the two men had a stubby, sandy-colored beard. He was lanky, making the *sombrero* he wore look bigger than normal. He picked his teeth with the stem of a match. He gripped a sawed-off, double-barreled shotgun in his other hand.

The third man—Fargo guessed his age wasn't over

twenty-one—stood at the liquor cabinet, swilling from a bottle of amber liquid. He was taller than the shotgun-wielder, and rawboned, with a lantern jaw. In his long scabbard, rested the deer-foot handle of a knife.

Bad Addie lay on the couch Fargo had occupied earlier. A tall woman, she had auburn hair, cut short like a boy's, and gray eyes. Her lips, however, were her most prominent facial feature. Bad Addie's lips were perfect in every respect. Under different circumstances, Fargo would have liked nibbling on them, especially the full lower lip. Slim hips gave way to long slender legs. Her left leg, bent at the knee, draped over the back of the couch; the right, extended straight, angled off the seat, and her boot heel rested on the tile floor. The pose was most sensual. A single bandolier crossed her chest. It held shells for a carbine that went unseen by Fargo. She also had a pair of Smith & Wesson army issues holstered. She was looking straight at the painting, behind which Fargo stood, watching through Don Diego's eyes.

Bad Addie drew one of the guns and aimed. When she squinted down the barrel and thumbed the hammer back, Fargo stepped to one side. He heard her say, "Bang, bang," then laugh and comment, "Hey, *seen-yore, I make seen-yore-eeta* out of you, *sí*?"

Fargo moved back to the peepholes.

Don Diego entered the room from the foyer. In his hands were a wad of bills. Handing them to Leonard, he said, "It's all there. You said five hundred, didn't you?"

Nodding, Leonard counted it to make sure Diego hadn't cheated him. Satisfied, he tucked the money inside his shirt, then drove a fist into Diego's stomach. Leonard growled, "We'll be back later to get more."

Rodríguez doubled over and fell to the floor. Leonard motioned the others to follow him out of the room.

Fargo watched them go into the foyer, heard Leonard yell for the others to hurry up and come on. After several moments three men came down the staircase, one stuffing in his shirttail.

María touched his cheek and whispered, "Come, I must go help with Papa."

Her fear of the gang of desperadoes completely overwhelmed her quest of sex. Fargo knew that now. Oh, she would go through the motions of sex, but like sucking on grapes, it would be nothing more than show rehearsed in front of mirrors. He said, "Lead the way."

The Trailsman silently vowed he'd come back to fight it out with the gang after he went to Austin. He'd taken Senator Winston's money. Like it or not, the man had first call on Fargo's services.

He moved back from the peephole.

María knew the black passageway well. She moved through the maze quickly, not unlike a rat might, up and down steps suddenly there. Fargo was amazed by her blindfolded memory. She halted abruptly. A narrow shaft of early-morning light flooded through the gap. She swung the bookcase out by an inch and put her eye to the slot. Several heartbeats passed before she pushed the bookcase straight out. She motioned Fargo to precede her. When he stepped into the bedroom, she said, "I'm going to my room to dress. Meet me downstairs." She swung the bookcase shut.

Fargo was pulling on his shirt when a woman in an upper-level room started screaming. Quickly, he pulled on his Levi's and grabbed his Colt. Outside, he looked down the wide corridor, left and right. The scream seemed to come from everywhere, then he isolated it and ran left. As he rounded a corner, the screams grew louder. They came from behind the second door on his right. He rushed inside.

María sat on the floor, clutching and rocking the tiny maid's nude, lifeless body. The maid's throat lay open. Blood covered María's naked body. She wailed, "Precious Dulce. Oh, my sweet, what will I do now?"

Seeing there was nothing he could do, he left them there and went back to his room and finished dressing.

Downstairs, he looked in on Don Diego. Teresa was helping him to his feet. Fargo stood at the doorway and spat venomously, "Now will you arm them?"

Husband and wife stared blankly at him.

Shaking his head, Fargo went outside to find his stallion.

Saddling the Ovaro, Fargo silently once again vowed he'd come back and have it out with the gang. But first there was the urgent matter in Austin.

The Trailsman rode east.

# 4

The torrential downpour had turned the thin layer of topsoil above the thick strata of caliche into a quagmire. The river still flowed out of its banks. But the morning sky Fargo rode under was clear. The heat waves were missing. So were the dust devils. They were replaced by a new form of torture: unbearably hot, humid air. Fargo's clothes clung to him like leeches. The Ovaro's plodding hooves unavoidably splattered mud all over his body. Neither the stirrups nor Fargo escaped the flying mud. His boots and legs were covered with it. The air reeked with the oily smell of creosote.

By noon the baking sun had evaporated enough of the water in the soil to change it to thick black goo. Globs of it clung to the Ovaro's legs and belly, Fargo's boots and pant legs. Progress was slow in the muck. The pinto's hooves left ankle-deep post holes every step he took. Fargo glanced behind at the tracks.

Slowly the goo thickened and the Ovaro found it easier to walk on. By sundown the mud was firmer. Fargo halted next to a stream that flowed lazily. He got a good night's sleep. He was becoming accustomed to the creosote odor.

Shortly before daybreak he eased into the saddle and changed course to east-southeast. He made good time for two days. In midafternoon the scenery took on a dramatic, welcome change in appearance. The flat landscape ended abruptly at the erratic edge of a cliff. He reined to a halt and gazed across lush green rolling hills complete with scrub oak, juniper, and green mesquite. A meandering stream traced along the contour of the cliff at its bottom. Here, there were no rippling heat waves or bothersome dust devils or smells of creosote. The air was fresh and clean. A cool breeze kissed his face.

He maneuvered the Ovaro down the steep cliff to the stream. The stallion entered it willingly. Fargo undressed, bathed, and washed his mud-caked clothes. Laying them on a bush to dry, he went back into the stream, to the Ovaro, and got his dandy brush out of his saddlebags. For the next hour he cleaned the stallion until his coat gleamed again. Then he sat on the bank to scrub mud off his boots, saddle, and tack. The brown-black stuff was everywhere.

After an hour's nap, he dressed, made the Ovaro ready for the trail, and rode onward.

In late afternoon three days later, he rode into Austin. The city was a beehive of activity. The streets were filled with buckboards and pony carts. A three-spring grocery wagon rumbled past him. A lanky kid snapped the reins and threw him a wink. Fargo counted five Studebaker farm wagons parked in front of a large feed store. Two young boys were loading a glass-window delivery wagon in front of Miller's Grocery Store. Pedestrians crossed back and forth to places of business. Among it all stood the state capitol building, surrounded by a sea of black surreys. Fargo rode to it and hitched the Ovaro to a post.

He'd been in state capitols before, so the massive interior and the smell inside were old hat to Fargo. Like on the streets outside, people filled the halls. About half wore derbies and smoked long cheroots, drummers looking for a deal that would give them a shovel and access to the state treasury. They moved in quick steps and smiled a lot. The other half wore clean cowboy hats and strolled to wherever they were going. Fargo found Senator David Winston's office and went inside.

A prim, no-nonsense schoolmarm type greeted him from behind her desk behind a mahogany barrier. Fargo felt unwanted. Her gaze scanned the full length of his body. In a high-pitched voice the woman snapped, "Senator Winston is in session. If—"

Fargo interrupted to ask, "When is the senator expected?" He removed his hat and slouched as though he were dog-tired.

The gambit didn't phase her. She squinted green eyes at him and said caustically, "Young man, don't interrupt when I'm speaking. I was about to say, if you care to wait, the senator will arrive presently. Do you have an appointment? Senator Winston sees by appointment only. He's a very busy man."

"I'll wait, ma'am."

"Do you have an appointment?" she persisted.

"Kind of." He sat in one of the four not-so-comfortable wooden chairs and put his hat back on.

She snorted, "Well, I do declare," and went back to shuffling papers.

Ten minutes later a husky man in his fifties strode into the office and barreled through the swinging door in the barrier. Crossing to his office door, he told her in a rich baritone voice, "The Potts-Blaylock bill was soundly defeated."

She picked up a notepad and pencil and followed him inside. Fargo's wild-creature hearing caught what she muttered to her boss. "There's a dirty cowboy waiting to see you. I asked if he had an appointment. He said, 'Kind of.' Do you want me to—"

Fargo interrupted from the doorway, "I'm Skye Fargo, the Trailsman."

The secretary stiffened and blanched. She whined, "Well, of all the nerve. Mister—"

"That's enough, Inez," Winston broke in. "Mr. Fargo holds an open appointment." Winston came from behind a cluttered desk and extended his right hand. "Glad you're here. What kept you?"

Fargo grasped his hand. Winston had a tight grip. Fargo liked him at once. He grinned, "West Texas. It's murder."

David Winston laughed. "Never been there myself, but I'm told it is a living hell."

Inez gasped, spun, and hurried out of the office.

Fargo nodded toward Inez. "The woman's a damn good watchdog."

"I yanked her out of a one-room schoolhouse down in Goliad six years ago. Been my keeper ever since." The senator pulled a timepiece from his watch pocket, glanced at it. "Give me an hour to round everybody up and get them in place. In the meantime you look thirsty. You'll find Clancey O'Toole's saloon down the street. I'll join you there."

Fargo nodded. They shook hands again and he left. He paused behind Inez and kissed her cheek.

Flustered, she stammered, "Well, I, I, I—"

"Do declare," Fargo interrupted her for the third time, "that's the best peck I've had in a long time."

Her hands came up to her bosom. She glanced at him and blushed.

Fargo sent her a wink, tipped his hat, and ambled out of the office. He spotted Clancey O'Toole's place easy enough: a white two-story structure with huge emerald-green four-leaf clovers at either end of the words SHAMROCK SALOON. A run-around balcony also served as the roof of the front porch. Lively piano music spilled through the doorway. Fargo entered and stepped to the long bar. He ordered a glass of bourbon.

Fargo watched all the activity in the long mirror behind the bar. A group of men watched the wheel of fortune spin. It clacked to a stop on a one-dollar bill. A loud voice cried, "Aw, shit! Missed again."

Saloon girls dressed in fancy clothes mingled with the customers. He watched a slender brunette pat a drummer's butt. The drummer stood at the crap table near the wall opposite the bar. Without looking, he batted the brunette's hand away.

There was a long table filled with food at the rear of the saloon. Fargo sipped from the glass as he threaded his way through the noisy crowd and went to it. A powerfully built man spun and bumped into him. His and Fargo's drinks sloshed onto the Trailsman's shirt.

The man shouted, "You clumsy ass, watch where you're going."

Fargo felt like hitting him in the mouth. Instead, he offered to buy the man another drink. The fellow snorted, "Humph!" and walked away. Fargo continued to the food-laden table. He munched on a pickle while assembling a ham-and-cheese sandwich.

The brunette appeared next to him. She said, "Hello, handsome. You're new in town, aren't you? My name's Gertrude, but you can call me Gertie. Anytime Gertie, that's what they call me." She smiled.

Up close he saw what she meant. By any name, Gertrude's mileage far exceeded her age. It showed in her face, especially around the eyes, and her hands weren't all that steady. He reckoned Anytime Gertie was twenty-five going on forty-five and running out of steam. He said, "Mine's Skye Fargo. And, yes, I'm new in town."

Anytime took a bite of cheese, then flipped the uneaten part back onto the stack. "Where're you from, cowboy?"

He knew she wasn't interested, so he said, "Around."

She looked at his empty glass, then to his wet shirt, "Want me to get you a refill?"

"Bourbon."

She took the uneaten piece of cheese with her. Eating his ham-and-cheese, he watched her go to the bar. The guy who had sloshed the drinks stood next to her. While the bartender refilled Fargo's glass, the brawny man grabbed Anytime's ass and squeezed. Even from Fargo's distance he could tell the squeeze was hard enough to hurt. Anytime turned and slapped him. The guy guffawed.

She brought the glass to Fargo. He saw she was bristling mad. "Did he hurt you?"

"Naw," she answered. "I'm used to Deavers." She snatched up an olive and popped it in her mouth. "Want to visit my room?" she asked.

Fargo shook his head. "Not enough time, Anytime. I'm meeting someone." He smiled. "I bet you'd be a hellcat in bed, though."

"Maybe later, then?" she asked hopefully. Again, she saw his head shake. Anytime shrugged and walked away in search of a horny man.

Fargo moved to the crap table to spectate while finishing the sandwich. The man throwing the dice was on a roll. Fargo heard somebody say he'd made eleven straight passes. A crowd had gathered to watch. A chorus of "Oh, my Gods" roared when he made his twelfth point. Money was all over the table.

Somebody jarred Fargo's right elbow. His drink spilled onto the back of the man he stood behind. The man turned and scowled at Fargo. Fargo glanced behind only to see that Deavers had caused the spillage.

The man snarled, "Want to make something out of it, cowboy?"

"Rub me wrong the first time," Fargo began, "and it's your fault. Rub me twice and it's my fault." Fargo backhanded him, saying, "And I'm not a cowboy."

Deavers recoiled from the hand blow. Blinking through watery eyes, he dragged the back of his hand across his bloody mouth. Fargo watched Deavers' tongue circle over his teeth to check for security. Deavers swung a left hook.

Fargo stepped back and blocked the onrushing hamlike fist.

The crowd instantly parted to make room for the two brawlers.

Fargo countered with a hard blow to Deavers' abdomen. He absorbed it without so much as a grunt. "I eat weaklings like you," Deavers growled. He began jabbing, setting Fargo up for the kill.

Fargo ducked and dodged the pistonlike jabs. One glanced off his right shoulder, the next found his jaw. Swirling purple-white stars filled Fargo's skull. Dazed, he covered up and shook his head.

Deavers' big fists slammed against Fargo's hands. Then they moved down and hammered his chest. That was a mistake on Deavers' part. The man was toying with Fargo, showing off to the crowd. Fargo's chest was the strongest part of his body. Deavers' blows on it meant nothing. Fargo used the time to clear his head of the fuzzies. Then he retaliated.

Fargo faked a left hook. Deavers dodged from it and caught the serious right. His jawbone crunched as his head snapped around. Fargo plowed his left fist into the stunned man's gut. This time he gasped and doubled over. Fargo moved Deavers head into position. He threw an uppercut that broke Deavers' nose. Then he straightened him up, pushed him, and Deavers fell straight back, unconscious before he met the floor.

The crowd applauded and whistled. Anytime rushed to kiss Fargo. Many glasses were held out for him to take. In his peripheral vision, Fargo saw David Winston. He sat with his back to a poker table. His legs were crossed and he held a drink, which he raised in a toast to Fargo.

Fargo peeled Anytime from around his body and went and sat at the senator's table.

Nodding toward Deavers' unconscious form, Winston commented, "Should've happened a long time ago. The man's a nuisance. Clancey's thrown him out at least a dozen times for molesting the saloon girls. He keeps coming back for more."

Fargo nodded and asked, "Why did you send for me?" He placed Winston's expense money on the table.

Winston said, "No, no, keep the cash. I meant for you to have it, regardless."

"Regardless of what?" Fargo asked. He watched the senator toss down most of his whiskey.

"Regardless of whether or not you accept the assignment," Winston answered evenly.

"What is the assignment?" Fargo pursued.

He thought Winston was going to tell him. He was wrong. Instead, Winston said, "By the time we get to the house, the others will be there. I want you to hear what they have to say. Are you ready to leave?"

Fargo answered by rising from the chair. He gestured for Winston to lead the way.

The senator went to a surrey. An elderly black man sat on the seat, waiting patiently, holding the reins loosely. Winston asked Fargo, "Will you ride with us, or do you prefer your own mount?"

Nodding toward the Ovaro, Fargo replied through an easy grin, "He'd think I'd turned on him, gone citified. I'll ride alongside the surrey and try to keep him off that good-looking filly of yours."

David Winston chuckled as he climbed to sit next to the black man. "All right, Buff, it doesn't look as though he wants a buggy ride. Take me home."

Home turned out to be an hour's ride. They chatted en route, mostly about Fargo's journey across west Texas. "I thought I had died and gone to hell," Fargo commented. "There isn't anything out there but greasewood and rattlesnakes." Fargo didn't mention what he found at the ranch, Río Pecos, or at Don Diego's. He didn't want to be a bearer of bad news.

Buff listened intently when Fargo told about the heat waves, dust devils, and the twister that had nearly snatched him and the Ovaro.

When Fargo fell silent, Buff spoke, "Lawdy me, Senator, I wouldn't want to be caught in that place, dead or alive. Uh, uh, no I wouldn't. Tell me again, mister, 'bout them waves what made everything look close."

It was obvious Buff had never seen heat waves. Fargo described them as best he knew how. Buff nodded lamely. Fargo felt relieved when Winston's homestead came into view.

Home? Fargo thought as he looked at the monstrous two-story stone structure. It's a small palace, he mused to himself.

Buff halted at the entrance. Alighting from the surrey, Winston suggested Fargo hitch his horse to the back end and have Buff trail him to the stable. Fargo dismounted. Tying the stallion, he told Buff to see that he got some oats.

Winston opened the front door and stepped inside. Fargo noted the mansion surrounded a beautiful courtyard with a pool in its center. Mexican tile formed paths connecting four entrances below a balcony that ran around the entire second level. Clinging ivy grew up the surfaces behind tall green plants. A man and woman sat opposite each other at a circular redwood table with six chairs.

Both stood when they heard the senator and Fargo coming. Winston introduced the woman first. Fargo removed his hat as Winston spoke. "My wife, Polly. Polly, meet Mr. Skye Fargo."

She smiled and nodded. Fargo saw the senator had taken the hand of a woman much younger than himself. He guessed Polly's age at thirty. A slender woman, she had fine facial features framed by tresses of auburn hair. A long, slim neck merged with graceful shoulders. Fargo returned her smile and nodded.

Winston looked at the man. "Will Garrison, here, is the mayor of San Marcos. Will's also an adviser to the governor."

Fargo and Will shook hands. A clean-shaven man, like Winston, his brown hair was flecked with gray. Fargo reckoned his age at fifty, a few years younger than the senator. Clear brown eyes met Fargo's lake-blues. A big man, Will Garrison stood as tall and straight as Fargo. And, like the senator, Garrison spoke in a mellow baritone voice. The hallmark of a good orator. "Glad you finally made it here, Mr. Fargo."

"Please, all of you drop the mister," Fargo stated.

The senator gestured for everybody to sit. A neatly dressed Mexican boy approached as they sat. He glanced at Fargo, then to the senator, who said, "The usual for me, Ricardo.. Fargo, what are you drinking?"

Ricardo looked at the big stranger. Fargo said, "Bourbon." Ricardo turned and followed the path to the door at the back of the courtyard.

The senator cleared his throat and said, "Now to business. Fargo, I know you're curious to learn why I marched you across all that hot country you have so aptly described as hell on earth."

Fargo nodded.

"Well, young man, we won't make you wait any longer."

The senator didn't know it, but he was doing just that. Fargo wished he would hurry and spit out the bad news. He'd concluded it was bad, otherwise Winston would have included it in his message.

Garrison blurted, "A gang is terrorizing—"

That's as far as he got before Fargo, wincing and groaning, stopped him cold. Running his fingers through his hair, Fargo lamented, "I knew I should've shot them when I had the chance."

"You saw them?" Winston asked in shocked surprise.

"Where?" Garrison quickly added.

"At Rancho de Sueño, Don Diego's spread," Fargo groaned. He told about seeing them through the pinholes.

Ricardo arrived with their drinks. Polly waited for him to leave then asked, "Really? From space between the walls? How ever did you get there? How did you see to find your way?"

Fargo muttered, "It's a long story with a sad ending." He wasn't about to give the details. "Suffice to say, I missed an opportunity."

Winston picked back up on the reason he'd called in the Trailsman. "You're probably wondering why the Texas Rangers weren't sent in to dispatch the Scoggins gang. After all, that is the reason the governor has them at his command."

Winston was dilly-dallying again. Fargo was ready to believe Winston would subject him to a recitation of the history of the Texas Rangers, from their inception all the way to the present.

Will Garrison saved Fargo before the senator could take another long-winded breath. Will said, "Truth is, two rangers were sent there at different times. Bud Walker rode west last November. Bud never came back. Neither was he heard from. So, Reeves was sent to find him and take care of the Scoggins gang. That was in March."

"The fifteenth, to be exact," Winston broke in.

Garrison continued, "Reeves hasn't been seen or heard from since then. Both rangers were good men, absolutely fearless in the face of danger."

Winston interrupted to repeat, "Absolutely fearless."

Polly looked at him and censured, "Please, David, stop interrupting. Let Will tell it. Please?"

Rebuked, the senator shrugged. He sipped from the whiskey while Garrison went on. "The rangers are presumed dead. David and I went to the governor and discussed bringing in an outsider, somebody who didn't wear a badge, somebody who is as trailwise and tough as a ranger. Only one man had the talents. You.

David sent the message to a hundred telegraph offices in the Southwest and West."

Fargo asked, "How many are in the gang? Where do they operate out of?"

Garrison spread a large map of Texas on top of the table. He drew an arc on it, then answered Fargo's last question first. "This area encompasses the areas from which we've received complaints."

Fargo was amazed by the large area the gang covered and said so. They had either taken control of a town to operate from, or—heaven forbid—rode from below the border. He asked, "Where do you suppose they go when they're not killing and raping . . . Excuse me, ma'am." He glanced at Polly.

"I know what they do," Polly began. "I've heard it told in most graphic terms."

When Winston mumbled, "Most graphic," she cut a hard stare at him.

Garrison said, "For the life of me, I don't know where they go. As you can see, towns and villages are few and far between out here. None has been reported as being the hub of their operations. While I don't want to believe it, everybody I've talked to says they go to Mexico, here." Garrison stabbed the pencil on a spot just below the border and said, "That's Big Bend country. The Comanche War Trail cuts right through it. Nobody in his right mind would dare get in their path. Besides, I've asked the Mexican government to check for Anglo activities all along their side of Big Bend."

"And?" Fargo inquired.

"They reported not one Anglo, certainly not seven, has been seen anywhere along this stretch of the border." Again he pointed with the pencil, adding, "Nor any evidence of them being there."

"You said seven," Fargo stated. "Is that all?"

Winston stiffened and broke his silence. "My God, Fargo, you make it sound like a pushover."

"Under the right circumstances, it is," Fargo replied.

Now Garrison answered Fargo's first question. "Yes, as best we have determined, the gang is composed of six men and one woman."

"Bad Addie," Fargo commented.

All three nodded. Garrison explained, "Adeline Scoggins and her older brother, Leonard Ray, are wanted in Missouri on murder charges. That pair left a trail of blood across the state before leaving. She's worse than him. 'Kill-crazy' best describes Bad Addie. She murders women and children as fast as she does men. She shoots animals too, for target practice, I'm told. Chickens, pigs, horses, you name it and she has been seen to shoot them. She's also a . . ." Garrison paused, looked at Polly, and said, "Pardon me, Polly, but he needs to know."

"I know all about the woman," Polly replied. "Please continue."

"Well, dammit, there's no other word," Garrison began nervously. "The woman is a slut. Not only does she, er, fornicate with her brother, she does it with the others. I know this is true because she's made people watch at gunpoint, including women and children."

Garrison paused to shake his head solemnly, then continued. "Leonard Ray is the brains of the outfit. Or so I'm told. Frankly, I think Bad Addie is. Anyhow, to name the others, Albert James, also known as Wichita, is wanted in Kansas for robbery and murder and rape. He cut a fourteen-year-old girl's throat after raping her. Clarence Dowd—"

"I know about him," Fargo cut in, "and his sawed-off shotgun."

"What you might not know is he used it on his mother and father." Garrison's eyebrows raised to emphasize his point.

"No, I didn't." Fargo admitted. "But I'd believe he did. Please continue with the rundown."

"Walter Arnst goes by the nickname Buddy. Sounds friendly enough, but he's not. He's wanted right here in Texas. Stabbed an old man to death. Sixty-two stab wounds, to be exact. None in the old man's heart. Buddy let him bleed to death.

"Then there's Alexander 'Alex' Pearsall. A nice-looking young man with an engaging smile. He shoots his victims while smiling.

"Finally, we come to J. C. 'Matt' Matthews, another young man. Matt's fast as hell with a six-gun . . . and good with it. He's known to have spun, drawn, and shot the eyes out of a man thirty paces away."

"That easy enough of a lineup for you, Fargo?" Winston muttered.

Fargo perceived that the senator was playing the devil's advocate, giving him the opportunity to back away from this assignment. But David Winston hadn't seen the buzzards stripping flesh off a rancher's corpse. Neither had he smelled the death Fargo did when he was in the house, nor seen the bloated bodies he found. None of the three had. He said, "From the first I knew it would be something special, not easy, and dangerous. Yes, I'm interested in this assignment, for reasons you people don't know about. Personal reasons. I accept."

They exchanged looks and smiles. Winston plopped a pile of bills on the map and said, "Trust me, there's a thousand dollars there. Take it, Trailsman."

Fargo fingered the money. He thought about all those heat waves, dust devils, greasewood, and tumbleweeds, not to mention twisters and rattlers. Slowly, he dragged the cash to him, folded it, and started to stick it in his hip pocket.

The senator scooted his chair back, rose, and said, "One other thing. You may want to back out after hearing it."

Fargo put the bills back on the table.

Polly said, "You have to agree to take a certain person with you."

"Who?" Fargo asked.

Will Garrison answered, "The Apache."

# 5

The Trailsman hadn't operated in consort with anybody else before. On the other hand he'd never gone up against this many ruthless murderers before, especially in open territory. Maybe an Apache would be of help. Apaches had endurance. He'd seen individual Apache men jog over one horizon of torrid New Mexico desert, cross it without slowing down or stopping, and disappear over the far horizon. Fargo reckoned he could use a second set of eyes and ears. He nodded and retrieved the bills.

Winston looked at Fargo. Fargo discerned that he was about to hear a profound statement. It showed in the senator's expression. Fargo waited to hear the other boot hit the floor.

Winston cleared his throat.

Polly said, "Tell him, David. Get it done and over."

Fargo glanced up at Winston. The senator shifted weight to the other foot and announced, "We want that gang brought back alive."

Shaking his head slowly, Fargo laughed. "Come on, Senator, you're asking the impossible. One or two of them, maybe, but not all seven." Will Garrison hadn't voiced his opinion on the matter. He seemed sane and rational. Fargo decided they knew something they hadn't told him about. Fargo asked Will, "Do you believe it's possible?"

Garrison nodded. He said, "Yes, Fargo, I do. The Apache's a bounty-hunter. A damn good one, I might add. The Apache is noted for bringing in outlaws so we can put 'em on trial, then hang 'em high."

"Then why don't you send the Apache? What do you need me for?"

"The numbers," David Winston answered. "The Apache has brought in singles and doubles, but never seven. You'll make the difference."

Fargo chuckled. "I want to meet this Apache bounty-hunter."

Polly and Garrison stood. Will said, "Step this way."

They led Fargo to the door on the left side of the courtyard. Inside, a tall man stood looking out a window. His ebony hair hung down his back to his rump. Narrow hips gave way to long legs. While the shoulders weren't broad, Fargo bet they would be powerful. The Apache was dressed all in black. A wide, flat brimmed hat having a low gambler's crown and a colorful Indian beaded hat band sat on his head. A long-sleeve shirt was beneath his plain leather vest. Matt-black spurs complimented polished boots. His gun belt rode low on his hips, the holster on the left, and was held down with thongs tied around his thighs. The handle to a Colt just like the Trailsman's poked out of the holster. Fargo estimated his height at six feet. From the back, Fargo reckoned the Apache was no older than thirty. When he turned from the window, Fargo saw why he hadn't removed his hat.

The Apache was female.

She nodded to the foursome approaching her. Black, penetrating eyes focused on Fargo. Her jawline was square, her lips were wide and full. High cheekbones complimented her narrow nose. Heavy eyebrows arched perfectly. Her soft red-brown skin was unblemished, the complexion clear. In a word, Fargo thought her lovely. So much so that he couldn't imagine her being a bounty-hunter.

David Winston said, "Isabel Sayas, shake hands with the Trailsman, Skye Fargo."

Those coal-black eyes reached into Fargo's mind through his own as Isabel gripped his gun hand. Her hand felt cool in his, not moist, and she had a firm grip. He said, "My pleasure, ma'am."

She replied evenly in a husky tone of voice, "Call

57

me what I am. Apache. What do you prefer me to call you?"

"Fargo."

Polly sighed and said, "Now that you two have met and sized up each other, shall we adjourn to the dining room?"

David Winston's left arm was draped across Will's shoulders. They were already going through an arched doorway into the adjoining dining room. Fargo followed Polly and Apache.

Polly determined the seating arrangement at the long table. The senator, of course, was at the head of the table. Polly and Apache sat across from Will and Fargo. Place settings were already there in front of them. They shared three bottles of French burgundy. Two young Mexican women served their salad under the scrutiny of a supervising middle-aged Mexican woman.

Fargo knew not to attempt probing information from an Indian, especially a female. Their answers, if any, were usually clipped to the point of being misleading. While they replied, they invariably did it in a way to cause a riddle, if not a true enigma, to result. Fargo had long since discovered the best and fastest way to gain information from Indians was to exercise patience while practicing the three L's: look, listen, and learn. Knowing Isabel Sayas knew this, he waited for somebody else to break the ice. Fargo ate his salad.

After taking a few bites of her salad, Polly opened the conversation. "Fargo, Isabel has a ranch north of here. It's quite large and beautiful. It's too late for them now, but earlier her fields were covered by gorgeous bluebonnets."

Fargo dared to probe, although in an oblique manner. "There's an endless sea of dry, blackened greasewood where we're going." He said it without glancing up to see Apache's reaction.

"When wet, it smells of creosote," Apache muttered.

So, she's willing to communicate, Fargo thought. And she'd been there, or heard about it. He nodded.

58

Garrison joined Polly and played the role of their intermediary. "Apache was born in Mexico."

Fargo nodded. "I've been there several times." He wanted her to know he was no stranger to the country.

Polly helped. "Do you speak Spanish, Fargo?"

"*Sí*," he answered, "and several Indian languages, but not Apache."

It went on like that throughout the meal, giving and receiving tidbits of information about themselves.

Finally, Polly asked Isabel if she wanted to go with her. Isabel nodded. They excused themselves and left the room.

Winston leaned toward Fargo and asked, "Now that you've seen Isabel, what do you think of her? Eh, Fargo?"

Fargo made his assessment as he drank from his wineglass. "She's an exceptionally immaculate woman. And impeccable when it comes to clothes."

"No, no, Fargo," Winston half-shouted, wincing. "Cut the crap. You know what I mean."

Fargo leaned back and replied, "I have mixed emotions about the woman. I don't know enough about her to pass judgment on her skills and cleverness, traits that are necessary on this assignment."

After a long moment of silence, Garrison spoke. "What, specifically, do you want to know about her? Perhaps between us we can enlighten you."

"Hell, I don't know," Fargo began. He sighed heavily, then continued. "I've never worked with a woman. But I do know they are different from men. You can't predict what they do, how they will act and react at the moment of a gut-wrenching crisis. Will Apache crumble in a physical contest, or will she fight?"

"Like a man," Winston answered emphatically. "I've personally watched her take on men half again her weight and beat them senseless with her fists."

"How about that Colt she totes? Any good with it?"

Garrison hurried to answer, "She has a target range at her ranch. Paints life-size silhouettes of men on planks, then backs off twenty-five feet or so and puts her back to the target. I've seen Isabel turn and draw and shoot from the hip faster that a striking diamond-back."

"Her target?" Fargo inquired. "Can she hit where she aims?"

"I went to the target with her and saw for myself. Fargo, I laid a silver dollar over that five-bullet pattern of holes. Yes, she hits where she aims. In this case, where the heart would have been in the man's silhouette."

"She's good," echoed Winston, and he added a new dimension, "with the Colt and with her bullwhip."

"She won't make love with you, though." Garrison mumbled the remark, then explained, "When Isabel was thirteen, four drifters raped her. They made her watch while raping her mother also. Then the drifters—all of them—killed her mother and father. They tied the naked girl to a tree and left her to die. All that happened in Mexico. Her mother was a full-blood Jicarilla Apache, her father a Mexican. Most Mexicans are part Indian, in his case half and half. More Indian blood flows through Isabel's heart than Spanish. That explains why she calls herself Apache.

"Anyhow," Garrison continued, "Isabel never forgot what they did to her and her parents. The images of the faces of the four drifters were etched in her brain. How could she forget them? She got her hands on a French-made flintlock pistol and went seeking vengeance. She taught herself how to load and fire the pistol while she tracked them down."

Garrison paused to take a sip of wine, then picked up on the story. "At age fourteen she found the first one in an El Paso *cantina*. She put the barrel between his eyes and threatened to pull the trigger if he didn't tell the whereabouts of the other three. After telling her Amarillo, she pulled the trigger.

"Isabel went to Amarillo. Walked all the way. One of them was actually still in town. He worked in a saloon. Cleaning spittoons and the like. She'd grown and her appearance had changed so much that he didn't recognize her. Isabel lured him behind the saloon on pretense she would screw him for free. He undressed. She pressed the flintlock's barrel to his family jewels and made him tell where to find the other two. He did, and she squeezed the trigger.

"The fellow said they had gone to Fort Worth. She walked there. By now Isabel is fifteen. She couldn't find them in Fort Worth. She thought to ask the sheriff. After describing them to him, he said he'd locked up both. They'd served their sentences and left town. The sheriff mentioned overhearing them talk about San Antonio. They had been released two weeks earlier. Isabel was getting close.

"She hitched rides to San Antonio. She started searching saloons and *cantinas* and found one of them on top of a whore. Isabel let him feel cold steel in the crack of his ass. After telling her his partner was on his way to Austin, she gave him a new butthole, and was on her way to Austin in five minutes.

"She had powder and shot left for only one more pull of the trigger. Isabel found the last man in Rick Dunsmore's saloon. She came up behind him, put the pistol's barrel to his head, and pulled the trigger, but it misfired. He beat her up. In the course of it, Isabel pulled a knife out of a bystander's sheath. She cut his throat wide open. Then ran."

Winston volunteered how she came by her ranch. "She worked at odd jobs until she was twenty-one. Saved most of the money she earned and learned how to speak English fluently. One sunny day this tall Indian woman appeared at my bank desk. Isabel Sayas insisted the bank loan her a thousand dollars to buy land and start a ranch. I was dumbfounded that she would even ask. But something about her indicated she was damn serious, and a good risk. Of course, the bank couldn't loan her any money. But I could. We rode out to the site she had selected. After seeing it, I personally loaned her two thousand.

"Best money I ever loaned. She paid me back within the year from money she received from bringing in outlaws shown on wanted posters. She went on to build one of the finest herds of longhorns I've ever seen. A big house, too. Not as large as this one, but as fine. Not bad for a thirty-year-old woman."

When Winston paused, Garrison spoke. "Altogether, Fargo, Isabel's brought in thirteen wanted men. Not one of them lay dead, belly-down in the saddle. That's why we call her a bounty-hunter. That's why we selected her to accompany you."

"Well," Fargo mused aloud, "she's damn sure earned the right to go. It will be interesting to see how this turns out, gentlemen. Interesting indeed."

The senator fetched a box of cigars. Handing one to Fargo, he said, "I have them special made in Cuba."

Fargo noticed the similarity to those offered him by Don Diego. He wondered if those Cubans didn't have a good thing going. After lighting and puffing it, he knew they did.

Polly appeared in the doorway. She told them that Isabel had gone to her room for the night, that she thought she would do the same. "David, don't keep these men up all night bragging on yourself," Polly continued, then reminded him, "You have to be in session at nine in the morning. Or have you forgotten? You want to be your best when debating these liberals. Don't linger. Please?"

"I'm coming, I'm coming," the senator capitulated. Pushing back from the table, he said, "Polly's right, gentlemen. I need a night of sound sleep before a dawn debate. If you gentlemen will excuse me . . ."

Looking at Garrison, Polly said, "Will, you know where to find your bedroom. Fargo's is across the hall. Please show him to it when you're finished talking. Good night."

Fargo watched them leave holding each other around the waist, then poured himself a fresh glass of burgundy. A moment's silence passed. Finally he said, "The senator mentioned his desk in a bank."

"He owns two. One in Austin, the other in San Antonio. He bought the one in San Antonio the same day he married Polly. I know you're wondering about their age difference. Polly is David's second wife. Margaret died of consumption in '52. David grieved for

**62**

more than a year. Then a Methodist preacher's daughter caught his eye. She had two sisters, one of which was Polly, who was away at the time of the budding romance. Polly came home shortly before they were to be engaged. The rest is history. Are you ready for bed?"

"No, not yet. You go on. I think I'll set here awhile longer."

"Your room is in the southeast wing. Can't miss it. It's through the sitting room where you met Apache. Stairs lead to the wing. Your bedroom is on your right at the end of the hall."

Fargo watched him down the remainder of the wine in his glass, then push back from the table. "Though it's none of my business, I am a tad curious to know something," Fargo said.

Garrison paused in his rise and asked "About what?"

"How much is Apache getting a head for bringing them back alive?"

Garrison stood to answer, "Not one penny. She's doing it as a favor to David. Isabel isn't slow to forget the personal loan he gave her at the time she needed it the most. Anything else?"

Fargo shook his head.

"Then, if you will excuse me, I'm going to get some sleep."

Fargo watched him leave. He finished off one of the bottles of burgundy, nibbled on a piece of his uneaten steak, then stood and blew out the tapers. He moved into the sitting room. Stepping through the archway to the stairs, he paused and looked at the courtyard door. The map was still on the redwood table out there. He decided to take another look at it.

Hurricane lamps lighted the four pathways. They cast light sufficient for him to see details on the map. He sat to study it.

A new fragrance suddenly appeared among those of the green plants. Fargo sensed somebody was watching him. His hand lowered to the Colt.

Apache stepped into view. He noticed she had just finished bathing. Her hair was wet. Tiny beads of water had collected on her forehead and upper lip. She stood on bare feet. The hem of her bathrobe touched her ankles, the collar snug around her neck. She sat next to him and looked at the map.

Fargo asked, more to open conversation than anything, "What do you think our chances are of finding them, much less bringing any back to hang?"

"Excellent. I've studied this map before. Made an analysis."

"Oh? And what did your analysis reveal."

"A pattern." Fargo watched her make an X. "It begins here," she said, "on ranches near Alpine." She entered April 4 beside the mark, then moved due north, made the next X, and logged in April 6.

Altogether Apache dated seventeen marks. The marks more or less created a semicircle that avoided Camp Stockton en route to terminating near Coahuila, Mexico, where the Rio Grande flows west to east.

She said, "I believe they go here." She touched the pencil's tip just below the border. "Boquillas del Carmen."

"I rode a straight line from El Paso to Austin," Fargo began. "I see no X at Rancho de Sueño."

"That's because they haven't reported the Scoggins gang."

He touched an X on his imaginary line. "Do you know this rancher's name?"

Apache nodded. "George Aikens. He rode to Butterfield's way station at Crescent Gap, here." She circled the area. "George asked them to report the gang to the Texas Rangers. You've met Aikens?"

"Not alive." Fargo proceeded to tell what he found at Aiken's place.

Apache suggested, "They either learned he called for the rangers, or told them he was through paying for protection. What did you find at the ranch?"

"It's owned by Don Diego, a cowardly man. The Scoggins gang came while I was there."

"You saw them?" Apache seemed genuinely surprised.

Fargo nodded. Apache listened intently while he

told about seeing them through Don Diego's eyes in the painting. He omitted the circumstances explaining how he came to be in the secret wall space. She didn't press for that information, but did in regard to his assessment of the individual gang members. After describing them, he mentioned each one's body language and temperament. He concluded by saying, "I agree with your belief that they hide out somewhere below the border." Fargo glanced at the map. "Doesn't the place where you suggested they go place them in the path of the Comanche War Trail?"

Nodding, Apache told him, "Yes, the Comanche go to Boquillas del Carmen to steal horses and capture women. Over the years the people there have grown to accept the Comanche's annual visits. The *federales* make it a habit to show up after they have departed. My guess is, Leonard Scoggins knows when the Comanche are approaching and leaves the little town in another direction."

"By now, Scoggins, his boys, and his sister have collected a small fortune. Odds are great they don't buy or pay for anything in Boquillas del Carmen. What do you think they plan to do with all that stolen money?"

While shaking her head slowly, Apache's eyes conveyed she was thinking. Finally, she admitted, "I don't know. The thought never entered my mind. What are your thoughts on the subject?"

Fargo chuckled. "After seeing Bad Addie and hearing about her, I wouldn't put it past her to gun down the whole lot of them in their sleep, then make off with the treasure. I don't know what she'd do with it, though. She's not about to change her life-style. None of them are." He started folding the map.

She took it as an indication he was going to leave. She asked, "Any wine left?"

They adjourned back to the dining-room table. He lit a taper. Apache sat across from Fargo and watched him fill two glasses. Sipping the wine, she reopened the conversation on a new subject. "I've never been any farther than where my Jicarilla relatives live, and then only as a small child. Tell me where you've been and what you've done."

For the next hour the Trailsman mesmerized her with descriptions of mountains and mountain forests, streams and waterfalls, the pretty flowers in the valleys, canyons and high country. He told of fights with Indians and outlaws, too many to remember. Fargo realized she had gotten him to talk about himself for a purpose. He thought he saw in her trancelike gaze that the Apache woman had left him. He said, "You want to hear more?"

She blinked and looked at him. "What were you saying? I was still in the valley of wildflowers."

He nodded. "I know. The valleys in bloom are the best part."

For what seemed a long time, they sipped the wine, lost in their own thoughts. Finally, Apache asked, "When do we leave?"

"If you're ready to ride, at sunup in the morning."

"Then I best get some sleep."

Fargo watched her stand and move to the door.

Apache paused, looked over her shoulder at him, and said, "I was the one who suggested to the senator that he call upon the Trailsman."

Apache opened the door. It closed quietly behind her.

Fargo had her approval.

# 6

They ate breakfast on a veranda that had an eastern exposure. Will Garrison came down last, sleep still showing around his eyes.

" 'Morning, Will," Polly greeted cheerfully.

Garrison looked at her as though her voice had passed through pea gravel. " 'Morning," he mumbled.

As he sat, Polly filled his cup with steaming coffee. She had two saucers ready and waiting for him, one larger than the other. They watched Garrison pour some of the hot coffee into the larger saucer and set the cup on the smaller. After blowing on the saucered coffee, he sipped it. The change was instant. Will became alert and civil. Looking at the sun half up on the horizon, he commented, "I'd say we're in for another hot day. Have you two youngsters decided when you're leaving?" He took another sip from the saucer.

The senator and his wife glanced at Apache. Isabel told them, "We head west right after breakfast. Will Garrison, how do you do it?"

"Do what?" he answered, surprised.

"Slurp coffee from a saucer without making a sound. When I try, I make more noise than hogs in a feed trough."

Will chuckled. "Takes years and years of practice. When my grandpa was teaching me how, my mother would leave the room. Polly, do you sneak a sip from a saucer when nobody is around to see and hear?"

Polly blushed. "Yes, Will, I do. With the same horrible-sounding results as Apache."

The two cook's helpers arrived with platters of food.

The cook observed from the doorway as they removed lids, revealing fried ham, scrambled eggs, biscuits, and red-eye gravy to pour over them. The veranda literally exploded in breakfast flavors. Fargo inhaled deeply and reached for a biscuit. Sampling the cook's red-eye, he saw the surrey come out of the stable. Buff held the reins. He took the surrey to the mansion's front entrance.

The senator said, "I must apologize for not seeing you off, but duty calls." He stood and downed the last of his coffee. Looking at Fargo and Apache, he told them, "Good hunting. Come back soon, bearing no battle scars."

Fargo and Apache rose and shook his extended hand. Apache embraced him warmly.

Garrison muttered, "Senators get all the luck."

David kissed his wife's forehead, then left, saying over his shoulders, "Comes with the job. *Hasta luego.*"

Polly explained, "The senate is having another ad hoc session to debate the pros and cons of what to do if war breaks out between the North and South. If it comes to pass, the senate is divided. About half argues to secede from the union. The others argue for a neutral stance. What is your position in the issue?" She looked at Fargo.

He wished she hadn't asked. He'd heard about the problem from settlers moving west and from others in towns and hamlets west of the Mississippi. Both sides advanced sound arguments supporting their positions. Not wanting to depart leaving a sour taste in anybody's mouth, he hedged her question. "Ma'am, I'm content to be a simple trailsman."

"Oh, come now, Mr. Fargo," Polly pressed, "even a trailsman can't escape having an opinion."

Fargo felt boxed in. All eyes were on him. Polly was forcing him to say something. "In 1850 there were only four hundred white people in the Kansas Territory. Today there are forty thousand. Both proslavers and abolitionist are hounding them to death over the same question you asked. Look toward Kansas to find your answer."

Garrison said, "Polly, he's not as close to the issue as we are. Don't try to draw him into debate." He glanced at Fargo and opined. "He wouldn't let you."

Apache lay her fork in her empty plate. She looked at Fargo. "If we're to make it to Fredericksburg by sundown, we need to head out."

He knew she wasn't interested in maintaining a time-table, only bringing the discussion about slavery to an end. He brushed his lips with his napkin, looked at Apache, and said, "I'm ready." Glancing at Polly, he added, "My compliments to your cook. She fixes excellent red-eye."

Polly nodded. They rose in unison and walked to the stable. The stable master, an elderly Mexican man, jolly to a fault, had obviously been watching the veranda and saw them leave it. A stable boy secured Fargo's bedroll behind his saddle. Apache's horse, a solid black gelding that Fargo estimated stood eighteen hands tall, was ready in all respects for the trail. A black blanket was under the black saddle, the bull-whip looped around its pommel. A lop-eared jenny stood nearby. The mule carried seven coiled ropes, twelve canteens, her black bedroll, cooking utensils, and food supplies. Fargo saw that during the night his saddle and tack had been dressed down, the Ovaro washed and groomed.

The old man noticed Fargo's observance. Beaming, he said, "*Señor*, you have a beautiful stallion. I personally cleaned his hooves and checked all shoes. Please make sure if you wish."

Fargo knew pride in workmanship when he heard it. The old man simply wanted him to see the physical evidence. Fargo lifted a hind hoof. The old man had indeed cleaned and trimmed it. "Excellent job," he complimented.

Pleased, the old man sighed.

"Where's my hackamore?" Apache asked him.

The old man glanced at the gelding's bridle and reins. Fargo noted the latter were adorned with silver buttons. The old man admonished the stable boy in

Spanish for the oversight and sent him to fetch the hackamore. By the time he returned with it, Apache had removed the other. Fargo saw the reason for the change. The all-black hackamore was void of anything that gleamed. Apache was heading into a sea of blackened greasewood and intended to blend into it. She didn't want a sunray or moonbeam to kiss off anything shiny to betray her presence in that black sea. Fargo's already good impression of her took an upward turn. He appreciated attention to little details like that. She stored the bridle and reins in a bag carried by the mule.

Nothing more was to be done. They were ready to leave. Apache stepped to Polly and embraced her, then Will Garrison. Fargo and Will shook hands. He thanked Polly for her hospitality, shook her hand, and eased up into his saddle.

Along with the old man and stable boy, Polly and Will followed them to the stable's entrance and waved good-bye. Slowly the sprawling Winston mansion disappeared from their sight. They rode abreast of each other, Apache trailing the mule. Little conversation had transpired. He'd heard her call the mule Lulu and the gelding El Negro.

When she spoke the gelding's name, Fargo muttered, "I wouldn't like being anybody's slave."

"Nor I," she replied. "The reason I never considered marriage."

"Nor I," he agreed, although he knew her reason wasn't out of fear of being possessed by a man, but forcibly violated by four. Fargo held his freedom to roam as sacred. Marriage was out of the question.

"Did you ever come close to a union?" Apache asked. "I'm sure that knowing females have tried to lure you into marrying. After all, those lake-blue eyes and chiseled face of yours, to say nothing about your size, would appeal to most women."

Fargo answered through an easy grin, "I reckon I did a couple times, when I was much younger. By the grace of God, I escaped in time. Been avoiding the wiles of conniving fillies, and mares, ever since. Yourself?"

She chuckled. "Tall women tend to attract men. They want to conquer the tall Apache woman. Take her whimpering to her knees, down to their level, so they can look her in the eyes. My height has plagued me from the beginning. It's been my worst enemy . . . and on one occasion, at least, a blessing."

Fargo dared dredge up bad memories for her. "You refer to the four men."

To his surprise, she was willing to talk about it. "If I'd been short like an average Apache-Mexican girl, they probably would have never sexually bothered me. They would have murdered me right along with my parents. In retrospect, my tallness for my age was a blessing. Three of them wanted to kill me. But one said, and his words still ring in my ears, 'Any bitch that can take the four of us without screaming once deserves to live. Leave the Mexican whore be.' The pain was great. I bit my tongue till it bled and suffered the ordeal. They should have killed me, too."

"I know. Will Garrison told me after dinner."

"Did he tell you why I went looking for them?"

"He implied that you sought vengeance for what they did to you and your parents."

She shook her head slowly. "Even at my age I knew the prospects of sudden, brutal death. I grew up in Boquillas del Carmen. My father hid me and my Apache mother whenever the Comanche came. They would've killed her on sight, taken me captive. We knew that. So we lived in the shadow of death and hoped they wouldn't discover us.

"When I watched the four Anglos murder my parents, I accepted it as their fate. I didn't enjoy doing it, but accepted nonetheless, believing I would also suffer their fate. I prepared myself for the inevitable. I prayed to God, asking Him to take them and me to heaven, and have mercy on the Anglos' souls.

"God saved me from my parents' fate. He put the words in the man's mouth: bitch and Mexican whore.

Then He gave me the resolve to track them down and kill them. I am not a bitch. Neither am I a Mexican whore. I abhor the words and will kill anyone calling me either."

"I too had traumatic experiences when young," Fargo said solemnly. "Only the circumstances were different. In my case there was no rape. The men simply came through the front door with guns drawn. They gunned down my folks. My father managed to shove me to the floor. The men must have thought me dead. Their bullets chewed into flesh and dug into the walls. I lay still and held my breath till they left, never knowing why they came in the first place. I can still recall the acrid smell of the gunsmoke they left hanging in the air when I rose and saw my folks' blood all over the room. Like yourself, I, too, vowed to find and kill them, and did."

After that brief exchange in personal histories, they fell silent. Shortly before sunset a stone house came into view. "We've arrived in Fredericksburg," she told him. Passing near the house, Fargo saw a farm wagon parked in front and three small children at play around it. Apache explained, "They're early. Normally the families don't come in from their farms to their *Sonde haus* till Saturday."

"*Sonde haus*?" Fargo asked.

"Yes, German for Sunday. Everybody around here is of German stock. Their Lutheran church is here in Fredericksburg. They wouldn't miss Sunday services for anything. Those who have farms farther than an easy wagon ride have a Sunday house. Normally, they are in them by sunset Saturday. Tomorrow they will flock in from all directions."

"Any hotels or boardinghouses?"

"Not a single one."

He presumed they would bed down on the far side of town.

She fooled him. "Good manners toward strangers passing through at sundown will prevent these God-fearing people from denying us feather beds. They will bundle with their children before allowing it to happen. You'll see."

Fargo was impressed by her guile and knowledge. The thought of sleeping in a feather bed appealed to him.

Apache dropped another boot. "Before you came down for breakfast, David told me you preferred bourbon. I took the liberty of sending a bottle of it to José with instruction to fill a canteen and mark it B."

Damn, he thought, this woman is amazing. She overlooks nothing. He said, "Wonderful. Your thinking about me is appreciated."

Apache laughed. "Remember, its the canteen marked B. Don't touch the one marked W. That's mine. Thought you'd want to take yours to bed with you."

Fargo looked at her anew. She absolutely, positively thought ahead. The tall woman riding next to him thought like a man. No! Better than most. Grinning, he shook his head.

"What does the head shake mean?" Apache observed.

"I was wondering if you tracked with the same attention to detail as you do in regard to everything else. I concluded you did."

"Get me there and you'll find out."

She reined to a halt next to a wagon in front of a Sunday house. "Wait while I go knock for a bed."

Fargo felt uncomfortable by her audacity. Hell, what did I think? The German farmers would hang out the windows and wave us inside. Apache made it sound that simple. She made no mention of begging.

Watching her rap several times on the door, he wondered whether under different circumstances, at the moment of a do-or-die crisis, her boldness would surface to save the day.

A stout, bearded man answered the door. A chubby woman looked around him at Fargo. Fargo swallowed his uneasiness. He touched the brim of his hat. He heard Apache say, "We are on our way west. We stopped to ask for a dipper of water."

The man studied Fargo for a moment while he fingered his beard and made up his mind. Finally, he stepped outside and pointed to a pump handle. Apache thanked him and started to the well. The fellow's *frau* whispered something to him. He looked at Fargo again and said, "Stranger, we can't take in both you and your wife for the night, but one of you will be more than welcome to stay."

Apache halted in midstride, turned, and smiled.

Visions of a feather bed loomed large in Fargo's mind. After all, he justified, there was a chill in the air.

The woman said, "Papa will speak to the Schmidts about taking in the other."

One feather bed was assured. Fargo gave it to Apache when saying, "Thank you, ma'am. The Schmidts will be fine for me." He hoped the Schmidts would balk.

"Wait for me to get my coat," her husband said, and stepped back inside the house.

Apache moved to Lulu and got the B canteen. Handing it to him, she broke a wide smile and said, "Sleep well, pardner. I know you don't like it, but their taking complete strangers into their homes shows their graciousness and generosity. Makes them feel good. Gives them something to talk about after church services."

Her words helped, some, but Fargo still felt uncomfortable. He nodded as the man came through the door. The fellow gestured for Apache to take her horse and mule behind the house, then followed her. He came back riding bareback astride a big draft horse.

He halted in front of the Schmidt place and slid off the horse. He banged on the front door. Fargo watched it open. A goliath filled the doorway. A slim woman appeared behind the huge man. The two farmers conversed in low tones. Fargo's wild-creature hearing eavesdropped. The woman studied Fargo while the stout, bearded man said, "They appeared decent, so Beth and I took his wife in. I told him I'd inquire at your house."

The larger man rubbed his nose while considering Fargo.

The shorter man helped him decide. "They're moving west. Be gone in the morning. At daybreak."

Fargo had second thoughts about letting Apache talk him into this fraud. He told himself he would gladly forgo the feather bed for sleeping under the stars in his bedroll. He called to the farmers, "No need to bother you, gentlemen. I'm used to sleeping out in the open."

The woman stiffened her back and called back, "*Nein*. Not as long as I have room for you. Papa, ask him to get off that pretty horse and come inside my house."

Fargo felt impressed by her discerning remark about the Ovaro. He touched the brim of his hat.

Her husband said, "Young man, don't you know an invite when you hear one?"

Easing off the saddle, Fargo thought it sounded more like an order than an invitation. He said, "Thanks for the hospitality. Herr Schmidt. You too, Frau Schmidt."

"Take your horse around back to the barn and put him with mine. After you're finished, come inside. No need to knock. We'll know it's you."

The bearded man thanked him. The two shook hands. The fellow climbed astraddle his draft and rode away.

Fargo led the stallion to the barn, watered and fed him. Reaching for the saddle's cinch, he hesitated. All of this was too damn easy, he told himself. Something cautioned him not to remove the saddle or anything else on the pinto. He had a strange feeling about entering this man's house. Fargo shrugged it off as nerves. But he didn't take off the saddle. Nerves go to hell—he trusted his feelings.

He went back to the door and entered without knocking. Frau Schmidt was setting her dinner table. Herr Schmidt sat in a big chair facing the hearth. He puffed on a curved-stem calabash pipe that was in keeping with his gargantuan size. Two females, their long blond hair gathered and braided in single pigtails, worked in the kitchen. Clearly, they were sisters. Fargo estimated the taller one's age at twenty, the other eighteen. Both smiled at him.

Frau Schmidt said cheerfully, "Come on in. Sit at the table. I'll pour a cup of coffee for you. Dinner will be ready soon. Papa, come visit with our guest."

The girls' eyes never left Fargo as he ambled to the table and sat. He believed he saw barely contained lust in the four light-blue eyes focused on him. He now knew what caused him not to unsaddle the Ovaro. He would have to be careful, very careful.

Herr Schmidt came and sat at the head of the table. Frau Schmidt filled their cups, then introduced her daughters. "Turn around, girls. Show your manners."

They faced Fargo, their hands clasped on their behinds. Both young women were well-fed.

When Frau Schmidt introduced Erika, the taller of the two nodded once. The shorter by an inch or two was named Heidi. She was also apparently prone to blush. Fargo saw soft pink blossom on her milk-white face when she was introduced to Fargo.

Their mother suggested they come sit across from their guest and talk with him while she finished dinner.

The woman didn't realize it, Fargo thought, but she had just turned the pair of lusting, big-breasted hens loose on the cock. They came willingly, if not eagerly.

In a tiny voice Heidi asked his name. "Are you a cowboy?" she added.

"No, ma'am. And my name's Skye Fargo. I'm a trailsman."

"What's a trailsman?" Erika asked. Her brow furrowed.

"One who searches where none have been before. A scout, if you will, and hunter of man and beast."

"Where are you going, Mr. Fargo?" Heidi asked.

He noticed Frau Schmidt pause at the stove to hear his answer. Herr Schmidt was curious, too. His head turned and cocked slightly. Fargo raised his voice a few decibels. "Don't rightly know, Miss Heidi. West for sure." Apache had said that after church their hosts would gossip about the strangers. He decided to color up that gossip. "The Apache I'm with, we're heading for the Comanche War Trail. Cuts through Big Bend country, a most desolate place. Only mangy coyotes, rattlers as big around as my arm, and scorpions can survive there.

Heidi gulped, "Comanche? I wouldn't want to go there."

"What Apache?" Erika asked, and her mother strained to hear his reply.

"She's staying with the, the—"

"The Walthers," Herr Schmidt muttered.

"She?" Erika mumbled. "You're traveling with one Apache woman? Why?"

"Looking for a gang of murderers. The Apache knows the lay of the land better than I do."

"Aren't you scared she might cut off your scalp while you are asleep?" Heidi wondered aloud.

"No," he said. "She's a tame sort."

"Lipan Apache," Erika stated.

"Jicarilla," he corrected for the benefit of the gossipers.

The food arrived and cut short their conversation. Fargo tasted the most delicious boiled red cabbage, German sausages, and boiled potatoes he'd ever put in his mouth. He complimented Frau Schmidt. She fidgeted and giggled behind a hand.

Her daughters' bare feet massaged the insteps and toes of Fargo's boots throughout the meal. When he challenged them with his eyes, all he got back were quick smiles and expressions of saintly innocence.

The mother and her daughters cleared the table. Heidi poured coffee for her father and Fargo, who remained seated at the table to talk.

"You mentioned a gang," Herr Schmidt said.

The curious females slowed washing dishes, barely disturbing the dishwater in the wooden tub. Fargo took a sip of coffee and began, "Seven of them. The worst kind." He proceeded to tell what he saw and heard. He also worked in a capsuled background of each gang member. When he told about the rancher's daughter, Heidi fled out the back door with her hands over her mouth.

Frau Schmidt gasped, "Oh! *Gott im Himmel, nein!*"

Herr Schmidt appeared astonished. But Fargo read

the man's expression wrongly. Papa said calmly, "They knew the risk when they settled there. A man takes risks, he sometimes pays a terrible penalty."

Fargo glanced past Papa to Erika drying dishes. Her eyes met his. She smiled naughtily. He looked away. He heard Heidi return, the females speak in whispers.

Frau Schmidt approached the men. Wiping her hands on her apron, she looked at Fargo and said, "The *fräuleins* and I are going to bed now. Don't stay up too late, Papa. Remember, we're expected at the Heinkel's barn raising by sunrise. When you're through talking, show Mr. Fargo to the spare bedroom. Good night."

Erika and Heidi breezed by Fargo and went up the narrow stairs. Before disappearing, Heidi paused, bent at the waist, and looked at Fargo one more time. He shot her a wink. She blushed and stepped out of sight.

Fargo turned to Papa and said, "I was prepared to sleep under the stars, which is what I usually do. I'm accustomed to it. Nature is my home. Isabel lives in a ranch house. She's more comfortable in the home. I fear we have taken advantage of you good people's hospitality by forcing our way into your homes. If you want me to leave, I'll go quietly."

Papa appeared offended that Fargo would suggest doing such a thing. Papa told him, "Strangers—the right kind, of course—are always welcome in our farms. Your Apache companion did the right thing, stopping at the Walthers'. You have to understand our way of life. We toil in fields from dawn to dusk five or six days a week. We rarely go anywhere except to our church. We don't have the time. So from time to time, strangers like yourself bring us news of what's happening outside our community. We repeat it many times after church services. *Ja*, you will sleep in a bed this night. We wouldn't have it any other way."

Sipping coffee, Fargo looked over the cup's rim at the stairs. He wondered how many other male strangers the farmer's daughters had visited in the spare bedroom. They had made it obvious that they had.

Papa pushed back from the table. He told Fargo

that a big meal always made him sleepy, and he felt tired and was going to bed. "I'll show you to your room. You can come and sit at the table and drink coffee, if you wish. There's plenty."

Fargo followed him to a door hidden in heavy shadows under the stairs. Papa pushed it open, stepped inside, and lit a lamp. Standing back, he said, "It isn't much, but you won't notice the cramped conditions while sleeping."

A window stood open in the outer wall. Six wooden pegs for hanging clothes jutted from the wall at the foot of the bed. There was no chair, only a three-legged stool. The bed was no wider than Fargo's bedroll, nor as long. And neither was there a feather mattress on it.

Fargo nodded. Papa set the lamp on a small table and backed from the room. Fargo followed him to the stairs. Going up them, Papa said, "You are an interesting man, Mr. Fargo, one whose experiences out on the frontier I admire. Sleep well, my friend. We rise early."

Fargo went back downstairs and poured a fresh cup of coffee, set the coffeepot on a not-so-warm spot on the stove, then sat to drink. Chuckling to himself, he wondered what sort of sleeping quarters Isabel got. He imagined her feet hanging over one end of a featherless bed and her head crammed against the headboard. "Oh, well," he muttered, "at least there's a window to gaze out of." He downed the remainder of his coffee and blew out the lamp.

In his room, Fargo stripped and hung his clothes, gun belt, and boots on the pegs. He slipped his Colt under the pillow. Stretching out naked, he nipped on the canteen of bourbon. The bourbon warmed his insides, relaxed him. Finally he set the canteen next to the lamp, propped on one elbow, and blew it out. The thin mattress was lumpy. He turned on his right side to face the window. Fargo drifted into sleep gazing at the stars.

A soft thud outside his window jarred Fargo's eyes

open. His gun hand moved beneath his pillow and grasped the Colt's handle. Thumbing back the hammer, he saw the vague form of a ghost drop past the window, its blond pigtail standing straight up over its head. Easing the hammer down, he waited.

Erika and Heidi peered over the windowsill. Raising a tad higher, he saw their smiles. Heidi touched a finger to her lips, cautioning him to be quiet. Fargo propped on one elbow again and watched her crawl inside. Erika followed. They wore billowy white nightgowns that hid nothing. Heidi walked by Fargo's bed to the door. Erika stayed on her hands and knees crosswise over his waist. Erika and Fargo watched Heidi put an ear to the door and listen. Fargo glanced at the big dipper and noted it was 4:00 A.M.

Heidi tiptoed to the bed. Looking Fargo in the eye, she pulled the gown up and off. Two perfect milk-white mounds the size of small cantaloupes punched out. Soft brown circles the size of four-bit pieces surrounded large reddish-brown nipples. Her hips curved nicely, and so did her slightly rounded belly. No bones showed. Fargo stared at her blond V. She smiled and whispered, "You want to go first, sister?"

Apparently I have no say in the matter, Fargo decided. He shrugged. "Why didn't you use the stairs?" he asked.

Again Heidi touched her lips. She told him to whisper next time, then explained, "Papa sleeps light. He has the ears of a cat. The wood squeaks in the hall and on the stairs. Papa would awaken and get his shotgun. Erika?"

"I'll go first," she whispered.

Fargo watched the older sister remove her gown and lay it over the lamp's flue. In the hands-and-knees position, her heavy breasts hung dangerously close to his left hip. Erika's left leg swung over his hips and she knelt straddling his thighs. Sitting on them, she began stroking his swelling organ.

Heidi knelt on the floor next to the bed and cupped his left hand to her right breast. Both young women rolled her eyes and moaned, "Uuhm."

Fargo concluded that they had indeed done this before. Theirs wasn't an extemporaneous routine; the second-story drop, the checking to listen at the door, the swift undressing, the no arguing about who would romp him first—everything they did were well-thought-out moves.

Heidi felt his biceps and pectoral muscles, bent and kissed his throat and shoulders. Fargo pulled her to him and kissed her, openmouthed. She moaned. He felt Erika get into position, part her hotness with the head, then pause. He reached a hand over Heidi and squeezed tenderly on Erika's left breast. At the same time he moved his other hand to Heidi's moist V and started rubbing on the upper part.

Erika raised her hips. The head entered. She squatted and captured half his length. Erika gasped, "*Mein Gott*, Heidi, wait until you feel this inside your belly." She squatted farther.

Heidi kissed his nipples, squeezed the chest and shoulders, sucked on his throat, nibbled his earlobes, bit his lower lip, licked his navel, and swirled her hot tongue in his ears. Both young beauties were in constant motion, Erika swaying on what impaled her, Heidi giving him a lip-and-tongue massage. When they weren't moaning their joy, they were whimpering or gasping it. When Fargo wasn't fondling their breasts, he was probing in Heidi's hot spot.

As though on a prearranged, silent command, the females suddenly swapped places. Heidi didn't fool around. She shoved her hips down and took in his full length. She gasped, "Aaagh! *Mein Gott, mein Gott* . . . *ja, ja, ja!*" She started bouncing on it.

Erika's open mouth found his. Stabbing with her hot tongue, she moaned, "Oh, oh, oh." Fargo pulled her up and buried his face in the silky-smooth, pillowy mounds, then nibbled both nipples.

The door burst open. Herr Schmidt's bulk filled the doorway. His flared eyes raged his fury. He roared lionlike. Erika and Heidi toppled backward onto the floor. Hands big as hams, gnarled fingers formed into twisted claws lunged for Fargo's throat.

Fargo rolled against the wall, stood, and danced away. Herr Schmidt's weight on the bed caved in its foot and headboard, cracked and splintered the sides and slats. A cloud of dust billowed up.

Erika and Heidi shrieked, grabbed their gowns, and fled through the doorway. As Fargo extricated himself from the bed's debris and the giant tangled up with him, he heard Frau Schmidt yell, "What happened? What happened? Heidi speak to me!"

One swipe of Fargo's left arm cleaned his stuff off the pegs. He grabbed his Colt and dived through the window. Tumbling on the ground, he saw Herr Schmidt trying to squeeze through the opening.

Papa Schmidt bellowed, "If I get my hands on you, I'll break your back."

You takes your risks, you pays the penalties, Fargo thought. The brute was hopelessly stuck in the window. Watching him struggle to get free, Fargo pulled on his drawers. Glass showered, the sill broke and splintered, and the frame ripped out as Herr Schmidt powered back and fell inside.

Fargo sprinted to the Ovaro. He charged out of the barn with the Ovaro in a dead run. Herr Schmidt rounded the front corner of the house, raised his shotgun, and fired both barrels. Buckshot whizzed over the stallion's head and peppered the barn. Fargo headed for the Walthers'.

He reined to a halt in front of the house and shouted Isabel's name. As he waited for her to appear, he pulled on his shirt. An upstairs window grated open. The front door opened. Apache leaned out the window. A sheet covered her body. The Walthers stepped out onto the porch. They wore nightgowns. Herr Walthers gripped a shotgun.

Fargo spoke to them first, " 'Morning, Mr. and Mrs. Walthers. The Schmidts sent me to remind you of the barn raising. Apache, get dressed and meet me about five miles outside of town, *muy pronto*."

"Which way?" she called back. "What's up?"

"West. I'll tell you later." He wheeled the Ovaro and pounded west.

Fargo met Papa about midway between the two Sunday houses. Papa was on foot, running, toting the shotgun. One suspender held up his pants. He was less than twenty yards away, in the middle of wagon-wheel ruts. Fargo was riding straight at him.

Herr Schmidt stopped and aimed the shotgun at Fargo.

## 7

Fargo's earlier experience with Papa Schmidt and his shotgun told him the man didn't give any lead, but shot straight at his target. Fargo was bearing down straight into the twin barrels. Schmidt would make mincemeat out of him. Fargo reined to the right sharply to provide Schmidt with deflection shot, and dug his heels into the Ovaro's flanks.

Schmidt swung to follow.

Fargo all but took the bit out of the stallion's mouth when he reined the fast-moving horse to a halt.

Papa squeezed both triggers.

Buckshot whooshed in front of the Trailsman.

Fargo gave the pinto a loose rein.

He dug his heels into the horse's flanks again. The Ovaro leapt forward and pounded away. Fargo moved the Ovaro back on the wagon path. "Aw, shit," he muttered. It occurred to him that he had forgotten the canteen. He stopped at the house to retrieve it.

Stepping from his saddle into the destroyed window, he saw Heidi walk past the doorway. "Ssst," he hissed between his teeth. She stopped and stared at him. "Come here," he whispered.

Heidi checked behind her, then stepped into the room. "Are you crazy?" she whispered.

"Are you? Bend over this windowsill and lift the hem of that gown. I'm going to finish what you two got started."

Heidi eagerly assumed the position. Fargo thrust hard and deep. Heidi started moaning, gasping. Her mother called, "Heidi, what's taking you so long?"

"Oh . . . oh . . . I'm coming, Mama. I'm comming. 'Aaaeeyii. Am I ever!" Heidi fell limp, draped over the sill.

Fargo withdrew and fetched the canteen. He pulled her off the sill, then went through the window and onto his saddle. Heidi's blond head rose over the sill. Her eyes were glazed and she gave Fargo a satisfied smile. He shot her a wink and headed out.

Papa ran to catch him. Frustrated, he threw the shotgun toward the Ovaro's vanishing rump. Fargo heard him thunder, "Don't come back."

He didn't intend to. The risks were too high. The penalties too great. He didn't halt the Ovaro until they were a good five miles west of the church. He finished dressing, then sat atop a smooth boulder to wait for Apache.

He watched the morning star fading out when she rode up to him. "Passing a house," Apache began, "I saw a brute of a man swinging a belt, chasing two young women dressed in nightgowns. They screamed their heads off. Earlier I heard a shotgun fire on the trail down from the Walthers'. Were the two incidents related?"

Fargo tipped the canteen and caught a mouthful of bourbon. He spoke evenly, as though dead serious, as though reciting gospel truth. "I don't know anything about how they got in my feather bed, or how that bed got busted, or the window next to it got torn out, or the giant and his double-barrel shotgun. No, siree, I don't."

"You didn't?" Apache said wryly.

"Yes, I did," he replied smugly. He held up two fingers.

Shaking her head slowly, Apache asked, "You got to sleep in a feather bed? Mine was cotton, thin and lumpy. My feet hung over one end of the bed."

Fargo chuckled and slid off the boulder. Mounting up, he told her, "German girls in these parts have been milking too many heifers. No, mine was a thin cotton, lumpy too. Didn't get a wink of sleep. No place to put my big feet."

They rode with their backs to the breaking dawn.

At sunset the third day out of Austin, they reached streams below the rocky cliffs. They unsaddled and removed the hackamore from El Negro and the reins from the Ovaro, then turned them out to water and graze. They started gathering wood and making a fire. Soon the still air held the aroma of coffee brewing. They sat and munched on beef jerky and red beans laced with green chilis—Apache's suggestion—while waiting for the coffeepot to boil.

Fargo's gaze moved up the cliffs. Oh, how he dreaded the brutally hot ride that would begin with the next dawn.

Apache noticed him looking at the cliffs. "I was much younger the last time I walked that land. I had a burning purpose then, one that was hotter than . . ."

When she let the sentence trail off unfinished, he looked at her. Apache's face was upturned. Ever-changing patterns cast by the flickering flames of the fire played on it. Fargo saw in those patterns painting her face: anguish, anger, determination, and tenderness. A tenderness unique to females only.

She blinked. "Hotter than the sun baking my brain." Reaching for the coffeepot, she continued, "I thought I'd never set foot on that parched land again. I still don't believe I'm really here."

"You're here, all right. Hell begins on top of that cliff." He held his tin cup out to her. "Will Garrison mentioned you are fast with your gun, and accurate. He also told me you bring wanted men back alive."

"I killed the first one. Did he tell you that?"

Fargo shook his head.

"Well, I did. And the sheriff in Lufkin didn't believe me. So I lost the two hundred dollars' reward and learned a big lesson. I started bringing them back for hanging."

He watched her stand, cup in hand, and pick up her bedroll. She headed upstream. Shortly, he heard a splash, then listened to her swim to the far bank, return, and get out of the water. He knew she wouldn't come back to the fire, but spread the bedroll elsewhere, out of his sight, always downwind of him. She did it out of respect. Apache didn't want to be guilty of tempting Fargo. He suspected that she slept nude.

He undressed, stretched out on his bedroll, and fell asleep staring at the stars. During the night a light drizzle drove him inside the bedroll. At daybreak the drizzle went unabated. They made their horses ready for the trail, forded the stream, and went up the cliffs.

At the top, Apache muttered, "Is this the wet side of hell?"

They laughed.

Intermittent rain stayed with them until shortly before Rancho de Sueño came into view. The many buzzards circling above the ranch foretold what they would find. Fargo unconsciously pulled his neckerchief over his nose.

Apache went to the stable and bunkhouse while Fargo checked inside the mansion.

Fire had gutted the once-grand house. Scoggins had also ransacked it. Charred furniture lay overturned. The glass front of the grandfather clock was shattered. Don Diego's portrait lay in shreds. A slender female arm hung down from the opening. Fargo began searching the house.

The pompous ranch-owner lay faceup on the dining-room table. Fargo reckoned the pudgy man had been dead at least three days. His chest was bullet-riddled. Black crusts of blood had formed.

He found the cook in her kitchen. She lay sprawled on the tile floor, most of her head missing. Her helpers had made it out the back entrance. They didn't get far. Bullet holes stitched across their backs. Fargo chased away buzzards, then pulled the young women indoors.

Apache met him on the stairs. She told him, "I've never seen such carnage. They didn't simply kill everybody, they used them for target practice. The horses too. Same thing in here?"

"Yeah," he muttered. "Let's go look around upstairs."

Teresa's twisted body lay in the hallway, the height of her fear frozen in her eyes and on her face. Fargo stepped around her body and entered his former bedroom. The bookcase stood open. Apache followed as he groped his way downstairs to the painting.

Sunlight spilled through the opening. María's nude body lay faceup on the floor, her twisted arm dangling over the bottom edge of the painting. Blood-spattered walls were heavy with the stench of rotting flesh. Her body had been torn asunder by a shotgun held at close range.

Apache peered over Fargo's shoulder. She gasped, "My God," spun, and ran.

Fargo crawled through the opening and dropped to the floor. He'd seen enough. Apache joined him on the front porch. Looking at the afternoon sun, he said, "Río Pecos is about an eight-hour ride. You want to leave now or wait till dawn?"

Without hesitating, she answered, "Now. The sooner we catch the bastards, the better."

Fargo nodded and stepped off the porch.

At ten o'clock they approached Río Pecos. Bright moonlight bathed the little valley. A coyote howled at the moon. No lights burned in the village. But they heard Manuel strumming his guitar.

"I don't recognize the tune," Apache said.

"It's 'Río Pecos Is Slowly Dying.' "

Fargo reined to a halt at the goat pen. The rails were down. He didn't see one goat. "Something's wrong," he suggested.

Apache looked down the narrow corridor, toward the sound of the guitar.

"We'll leave our mounts and Lulu here and go check on things," he said. "At least Manuel is alive," he added.

They dismounted and unsaddled the horses. Fargo walked next to one wall, Apache the other, their hands loose, an instant away from the grips on their guns. Fargo paused at the first hovel door he came to. Apache watched him nudge the door open with a boot. After looking inside, he shook his head. Apache checked the next two doors on her side of the hall and found the rooms empty.

The third door she checked was partially open. A woman's arm lay palm-up in the moonlight spilling in on the earthen floor. Apache bent and touched lifeless flesh. She rose, looked at Fargo, and shook her head.

They found nine other bodies before coming to the *cantina*. The door was wide open. Fargo stepped inside. Apache looked in. Ten bodies littered the place. The bartender lay over his bar.

"I told Don Diego to arm these people," Fargo began, "and suggested to Lucita that she and everybody else should leave Río Pecos. Come on. We'll go see why Manuel's still alive."

They followed the sound of the guitar to where Fargo had seen the priest laying out the lines of a mission. Manuel sat in a shaft of moonlight, his back against an adobe wall, his legs parted and outstretched. The young priest sat six feet away on Manuel's left. Had it not been for the bullet hole in the priest's forehead, Fargo would have thought him snoozing. The child Fargo had seen with Lucita's sister sat in front of Manuel, watching and listening to him strum the guitar.

Fargo squatted behind the girl. Manuel strummed a chord and stopped abruptly. He glanced up at Apache, but spoke at Fargo. "*Señor*, please take the little girl. Her name is Pilar Estrella. She is a good girl, *señor*."

Manuel lowed the guitar to rest on his thighs. Blood covered his waist. Clearly Manuel was dying. Fargo hugged the girl to him and asked, "Scoggins?"

"*Sí*, they came, too."

Apache echoed, "Too?"

"*Sí, señorita*, before the Comanche. Scoggins' men killed a lot of people after his sister collected all of our money. Twenty, thirty people. They laughed, *señor*, and said they were going to give Río Pecos what they gave to Rancho de Sueño. It was horrible. Everyone running, screaming, begging for their lives. Lucita? You remember her. Pilar's aunt. The man with the little shotgun killed her."

"The Comanche?" Fargo asked.

"After Scoggins left, we buried our dead, then most started wandering back to Mexico. The Comanche struck at sundown. They took our animals and women and killed the men." Manuel glanced at the priest, "Father Barra and I fought them. But there were too many."

"How many?" Apache asked.

"I don't know, *señorita*. They were all over the village, screaming, running, killing. It went on until dark." His gaze moved onto the girl. Blinking, he caught his breath. When he next spoke, the words came hard and in a near whisper. "The Comanche left at night. Río Pecos groaned in pain. By dawn, all was quiet. The roosters did not crow that day. I heard little Pilar crying for her mother. Take care of her, *señor*. Pilar is a good little girl." His eyes drifted up Apache's length and settled on her face. *"Adiós, señorita."*

Fargo watched Manuel's eyes close. His relaxed hand slipped from the guitar, the fingers dragging a final chord on the strings. Fargo rose with the girl in his arms. She looked into his eyes and smiled. He questioned Apache with his eyes.

"Don't look at me like that," she said grimly. "I don't know what to do with her. I've never taken care of babies or small children."

Apache was as ill-prepared to take charge of Pilar as Fargo. But they couldn't leave her. "Neither have I," he muttered. "You could learn."

Those black eyes of hers bore into his soul. "So could you."

He sighed and suggested, "We'll think of something."

"Something? What, for instance?"

"Hell, Apache, I don't know. Something," he repeated. "Let's go over to the *cantina* and light a candle. I want to look at that map again."

At the *cantina*, Fargo pulled the head bartender off the bar and sat Pilar on it, then he dragged the dead out into the street. Apache found and lit a candle.

Fargo opened the map and said, "We're somewhere in this general vicinity. Agreed?"

Apache nodded. He moved the finger left and up a way. "I found the ranch about here. I didn't see a damn thing west of there except cactus and grease-wood." His finger circled an area due north of the ranch. "Do you know of anything out in this part?"

She sat and pulled the candle close. "I believe the Butterfield Line cuts through there on the way to Camp Stockton. The line has a swing station in Crescent Gap."

Fargo looked at Camp Stockton and mentally measured the distance from there to Río Pecos, then did the same on an imaginary line north of the ranch. He concluded that intercepting a Butterfield Line stage would be closer. "How often does the stage come this way?" he wondered aloud.

Apache shook her head.

"Doesn't matter," he said. "They will have swing stations, places to change teams, every thirty miles or so. I know the stage doesn't run east to Río Pecos. Why don't we go north?"

Apache glanced to the bar. "Are you thinking about leaving the girl at a swing station?"

"Why not? She'd be better off. Lord knows we can't wag her around with us." Fargo folded the map and stuck it inside his shirt. He swept the girl up in his arms and took her outside.

They chatted while walking to the goat pen, Apache on one side of the tight passageway, Fargo with the girl on the other. He noticed Apache stayed in heavier shadows whenever possible. The all-black garb made her practically invisible. Looking at the girl, he muttered, "*Niña*, why are you so quiet? Cat got your tongue?"

Pilar shook her head.

Apache answered, "She's part Indian. More so than Mexican. You can see it in her face."

"So?"

"Indians teach their young from birth to be quiet. I'm surprised you didn't know that."

What Apache said was true. A crying baby pinpointed his or her mother for warriors searching for women. Fargo had traveled with Indians during the night. When an enemy encampment stood in their path, they didn't necessarily go around it. They would halt to wrap and tie pieces of blankets around their pony's hooves, then proceed. Not one sound came from the ponies or the children. He said, "I would think being reared in town made a difference."

"Habit," Apache replied. "An Indian mother is not quick to forget and break it. In all probability, the girl's teaching is what saved her life when the Comanche came."

Thinking aloud, he changed the subject somewhat. "Speaking of the Comanche, which way do you figure they went when they left Río Pecos?"

"South," she answered without any hesitation.

"And which way did the Scoggins gang go?" he countered.

"I don't know," she admitted.

"You heard what Manuel said?"

"No, not everything. You were closer to him than I was. Refresh my memory."

"He mentioned that Scoggins' men had said they were going to give the people at Río Pecos what they had given Don Diego. I take that to mean they went to Don Diego's place first."

"Then Scoggins is sweeping north."

"What does that tell you?"

Apache didn't answer until they were at the goat pen. "What does it tell you?"

Fargo stood Pilar on the ground and fetched his bedroll. "It tells me Scoggins and his boys are preparing to leave this part of Texas."

He watched Apache toss her bedroll onto the flat roof of the hovel opposite the goat pen. Turning to face him, she said, "Fargo, you amaze me. Really, you do. What leads you to believe that?"

Spreading the bedroll in the middle of the *corrida*, he told her, "First, Scoggins murdered everybody at Rancho de Sueño and ransacked Don Diego's mansion. Why would he do that? Why would he kill a good source of supply? Then he came here and did the same thing. Before all that, he murdered the rancher and his family. Scoggins had bled every cent, anything of value from the people on his route. His well has gone dry. It tells me he is making one final pass to glean what he can from the leavings. Then he will disappear."

"Makes sense," Apache replied.

He lay down on the bedroll and put Pilar's head in the crook of his left shoulder.

Apache pressed atop the roof. Opening her bedding, she asked, "What do you suggest we do?"

"Get in front of them."

Apache crawled to the roof's edge and posed the very question that bothered him. "Then, we best hurry. How do you propose we do that with the girl?"

"Our only hope is we'll get lucky and find a woman at the swing station, one who is willing to take her off our hands." He watched Apache shake her head as she retreated out of his sight. Then he looked at Pilar and whispered, "Are you really an Indian?"

She whispered back, "*Sí*. Apache."

He drifted into sleep wondering what he would do if there was no woman at the swing station.

Fargo's inner clock awakened his inert brain as dawn broke over Río Pecos. He eased Pilar's head off his shoulder and went inside the goat pen to empty his bladder. While relieving himself he heard Apache doing the same on the roof. He looked at Lulu and asked, "What do you suppose this new day will bring to us?" Another hot day, he reckoned. He buttoned up, then started making the Ovaro ready for the trail.

Apache's bedroll fell to the ground, then she dropped from the roof and came inside the pen. Saddling El Negro, she said, "I went to sleep thinking of what you said about Scoggins clearing out of Texas."

"And?"

"And I concluded that their nerves are wearing thin from being together so long."

"I agree," he replied. "Go on."

"Familiarity breeds contempt, even among thieves and murderers. I'd say Scoggins had his hands full holding the gang together."

"I think you're right. And?"

"The question arises: where do they spend all that money squeezed from Rodríguez and others like him? By now, Scoggins has amassed a small fortune."

Fargo chuckled. "And his treasure chest is overflowing with jewelry extracted from his victims, living and dead."

Leading El Negro and Lulu from the pen, Apache suggested, "They will fight over it. You know they will."

He roused Pilar and told her to get ready to leave while he rolled up his bedding. Securing it behind his saddle, he replied to Apache's last comment, "You're right, of course. It's in the nature of westerners to practice materialism and greed. It's safe to believe they'll end up killing each other to get it."

Pilar came back and held her hands out for him to pick her up. Fargo lifted her onto the saddle and told her to scoot forward, then eased up behind her.

They rode out of Río Pecos as the fiery rim of the sun peeked over the horizon. It brought a dramatic rise in temperature. Soon afterward the heat waves appeared, and the first of a legion of dust devils were born.

Two blistering sunrises later, a long mesa came into view. Apache told him its twin stood on the far side and Crescent Gap in between. "Butterfield follows the gap," she said.

Coming closer to the barren mesa, they saw a fast-moving trail of dust. At first Fargo believed it was caused by strong wind sucked into the vortex of the gap. He squinted through the shimmering heat waves and saw he was wrong. A stage trailed it. Surely there would be a swing station nearby.

Apache announced, "Have you spotted the two men on the mesa?"

He quickly scanned over it. "Now I see them." They were hunkered down on the ground beside their horses, facing the oncoming stage, which had disappeared behind the mesa. As Fargo watched, they mounted up and rode out of sight down the other side.

Soon afterward he heard the muted sounds of brief exchanges of gunfire. He suggested Apache take the girl while he rode ahead to see what was going on. Instead, she slipped the rope trailing Lulu, spurred El Negro into a hard run, and left Fargo blinking at her dust.

# 8

Coming into Crescent Gap, Fargo saw the stage had stopped. Four men stood at the left rear of it. The wheel had come off. He didn't see Apache.

Approaching the stage, he saw it was a celerity, designed by John Butterfield himself. John's design took into account the landscape found between St. Louis on one end of the 2,750-mile route the line traveled and San Francisco at the other end. Butterfield sacrificed springs and used thoroughbraces instead to drop the vehicle's center of gravity required for rough terrain. This resulted in giving the celerity a constant swaying motion, the reason for passengers' complaints that they felt seasick. Fargo detested riding in one of them.

The axle had carved a long rut in the ground before the driver managed to halt his team of horses. Fargo dismounted and added his muscles to the others raising the celerity high enough to put the wheel back in place.

Finished, they stood back and introduced themselves. Fargo shook hands with the sweaty driver, who said, "Thanks, mister, we needed your strength. Name's Carl Stadum." Carl's eyes moved from Pilar to Lulu, then back to Fargo.

"Mine's Skye Fargo."

"And mine's Rusty Eubanks." Smiling, Rusty stuck out his hand.

Moving from right to left, Fargo learned the other two were named Ethan Finlay and George Rogers. George was going to El Paso, Rusty and Ethan all the way to San Francisco.

Citing their names and destinations didn't make a damn to Fargo. More urgent matters were foremost in his mind. He looked at Carl and asked hopefully, "How far to the next way station? Is there a woman there?"

He watched them exchange quick glances. Their expressions clearly implied they were in the presence of a sex-starved man, and a big, powerful one at that.

All four men shifted their weight from one to the other foot. Carl and Rusty rubbed their faces. George and Ethan just stared at the ground.

Carl grunted, "Uh, what do you mean?"

Fargo changed the subject. "What in the hell happened here, anyhow? I heard gunfire and came as fast as I could. Have you seen my partner?"

Carl cocked his head and squinted one eye at Fargo and said, "Mister, we don't have one penny left. Two outlaws chased us down and robbed us. They got all we had. In answer to your last question, after they rode off yonder way . . ." Carl paused and pointed across the gap. Looking back at Fargo, he went on, saying, "A rider in black clothes and astride a black stallion thundered after them. Went by so fast we hardly got a glimpse of him. Was he your partner or another outlaw?"

"She," Fargo corrected.

"She?" Rusty echoed.

Again they exchanged quick glances and shifted their weight.

Fargo explained, "Some call me the Trailsman. The rider you saw on the black stallion is an Apache bountyhunter, a rancher near Austin, Texas. We're hunting for the Scoggins gang of outlaws." He went on to tell them what they found at Rancho de Sueño and Río Pecos. "That little girl sitting in my saddle is the sole survivor," he said. "Now, we can't chase down Scoggins with the girl. She'd get in the way. That's why I asked if there was a woman at the next station. Maybe she'd be willing to take Pilar off our hands."

"No," Carl began, "there aren't any womenfolk anywhere on the Butterfield Line. Sorry."

"Damn," Fargo muttered, his hopes dashed. In a stronger voice he said, "Apache will be along in a minute or two. You gents want to wait and get your money back, or go on?"

George answered, "What makes you think that woman will catch them?"

Fargo chuckled. "Want to wait and see?"

Carl was of the opinion that they had tarried long enough as it was. He said, "Boys, I'm running late. Mr. Butterfield runs a tight schedule. I'm for going on."

Rusty countered, "I lost two hundred dollars and a gold watch. I'm for waiting. You, Ethan?"

Before Ethan could answer, George spoke, "They missed finding the hundred I had in my left boot. But I'll wait if the majority wants." He looked at Ethan.

Fargo spotted Apache the instant she topped the mesa on his right. El Negro trailed two horses bearing two riders, belly-down across their saddles. "I suggest you wait," he told them, nodding toward the slope.

They followed his line of gaze. Ethan mumbled, "Well, I'll be damned if she didn't catch 'em. Mister, you've saved me four hunnert dollars."

"No," Fargo corrected, "Apache did."

They watched her ride in and rein to a halt. Sitting easy in the saddle, Apache pushed back her hat, glanced over her shoulder at the two outlaws, and said, "They're out cold. They made the mistake of staying together."

Fargo recognized Hank Tyler's chaps before lifting his head. The other was Cooney Roberts. Both were tied hand and foot. Fargo pulled them from their saddles onto the ground and said, "All right, men, you can go through their pockets. Take only what you gave up."

While they were doing it under the watchful eyes of Fargo, Apache dismounted and went to Lulu. She brought back a notepad and pencil, saying, "I need a written and signed account of what happened here. I'll take them back to Austin and turn them over to Sheriff Walker. Which one of you is the driver?"

Carl stepped forward. She handed him the pad and

pencil and instructed, "In your own words state the time and place and what happened. Then sign it and have the others do the same."

While Carl was busily scribbling, Fargo asked her, "They don't have a mark on them? How did you do it?"

She shook her head slowly, grinned, and said, "Robbers, they are. Clever, they aren't. When I caught up to them, they were off their horses, counting the money. Their backs were to me when I rode up. I was on them before they knew it. You should have seen the surprised look on their faces when they spun to face me. They made the mistake of drawing down on a gun already pointing at them. I shot both pistols out of their hands. They started yelling and dancing a clumsy jig. I rode up and slapped both up aside the head. Easy."

Fargo chuckled.

Apache looked at Pilar. "How about the girl?" she asked.

Fargo shook his head, answering, "No luck. Carl tells me there aren't any women at the swing stations or *posadas*. So, I guess we'll have to keep her a mite longer."

The pair of outlaws stirred and caught Fargo's attention. "Wake up, Cooney," he said. "You, too, Hank."

Groaning, they rolled over and stared at him groggily. He waited for each to bring him into focus, then said, "So, we meet again." Fargo smiled down at them. "You two turkey buzzards are going to be the laughingstock of the jailhouse when the other prisoners hear you let a woman bring you in without putting up a fight."

They looked at Apache. Cooney gasped, "A woman? That's a woman?"

Fargo thought they were fixing to cry. Pained expressions blossomed on their faces.

"Oh, shit," Hank muttered.

Carl handed her the notepad and pencil and said, "Everybody signed what I wrote."

Apache scanned over it and said, "Looks good

enough to me. Thanks." She tore off the top sheet, folded it, and stuck it in her hip pocket.

Carl offered, "The army has a guardhouse at Camp Stockton. You folks going that way?"

His implication was clear enough for Fargo. When he glanced at Apache, she said, "Why not? We can pick them up after we get Scoggins."

Fargo looked at Hank and teased, "Couple of scum like them? Why bother with dragging them to jail? I'm in favor of killing them here and now. You have the signed document that proves they're guilty."

Cooney pleaded, "You can't do that, mister. We ain't had no trial yet."

Hank whined, "It ain't fair."

Ethan gasped, "You wouldn't?" He stared at Fargo as though he believed Fargo would.

Apache said, "You're my prisoners. What I say goes. If you give us any trouble on the way to Stockton, I'll shoot you myself. Is that clear?"

Hank exhaled a mighty breath of relief.

Cooney answered, "Clear enough for me, lady."

Fargo released the pigging ropes that held their feet and said, "Climb up into your saddles, then we'll be on our way. I just might plug you when she isn't looking," he threatened in a nasty tone. Turning to Carl, he said, "That's it. You sure there aren't any womenfolk at the next swing station?"

Carl repeated his earlier comment, then told his passengers to get back in their seats and he climbed into his own. Fargo and Apache exchanged good-bye waves with the passengers as the stage pulled away. El Negro trailed Apache's prisoners while the Ovaro trailed the mule. Fargo and Apache rode beside each other. He muttered, "We already have a tidy collection and we're just starting. By the time we finish, we'll be trailing a small army of desperadoes."

Apache just looked at him and smiled.

A breeze blew between the mesas. No rippling heat waves formed in the gap, not one whirlwind did Fargo see. For that, he was grateful. But the instant they rode out of Crescent Gap, all this changed. Once again they became inundated by the broiling surge of murderous heat rising off the desolate terrain. Fargo removed and tied his neckerchief on Pilar's head and adjusted it just below her dark eyes.

After about an hour, he asked Apache, "Have you ever been in Camp Stockton?"

"Yes," she answered. "When I hunted for the four men. Back then it wasn't a military outpost. Will Garrison told me the army established a chain of camps about a year and a half ago. Camp Stockton was one of them. The army built the camp next to natural springs the Apache and Comanche have used for a long, long time, even before white men came. My mother told me that," she explained. "Settlers in the area complained about Indian raids so much and so often that the army was forced to come in and provide protection. But the army will pull out if war starts between the North and South. Garrison and Winston told me that. And they believe war is inevitable."

Fargo silently agreed. Moving off the likelihood of war and Camp Stockton, he asked, "How about where you were born and reared?"

"Boquillas del Carmen? It's probably the same as I last knew it. It's just south of the border at one end of Boquillas Canyon, a gorgeous place. There isn't much to tell about. Have you ever been in a small Mexican village?"

Domingo and Las Rocas flashed in Fargo's mind. He nodded.

She said, "Then you know what Boquillas looks like. It's larger than Río Pecos. Mission, Mexican Army headquarters—when they are there—everything. The Scoggins gang have probably taken control over the village . . . and the army, if you know what I mean. With all the money they have stolen, they can afford what little it takes to bribe the *federal* officer in command."

"Any pretty *señoritas* in that village you're talking about?" Cooney drawled.

"Shut your mouth," Fargo called to him. He didn't realize Apache spoke loud enough for them to hear every word. He loosened the trailing rope and added distance between him and Cooney.

At sundown, Fargo reined to a halt next to three parched-black mesquite. Before dismounting he scanned the flat terrain in hope of spotting signs of a stream or water hole and a place where they could relieve themselves, and saw none. He dismounted and asked Apache to take Pilar out a ways so she could squat, then told Hank and Cooney, "Get off those horses and follow me." When they slid from their saddles, he saw both had dark stains down one of their trousers legs.

Hank said, "I was afraid you'd kill me if I asked you to stop long enough for me to take a leak."

"Come on," Fargo replied, "and don't look back."

"Where are you taking us?" Cooney asked in a fearful voice. "What're you gonna do?"

"Quit asking so many questions," Fargo snarled. "You'll see soon enough." He slammed both of them forward.

Hank believed he was taking his last walk. He said, "Well, Cooney, I guess this is it for you and me. He's going to shoot us. I don't know why I let you talk me into all this trouble." He started running.

Fargo fired one shot in the air. Hank screamed and skidded to a halt. "Don't do that again," Fargo warned. He continued with them for another fifty strides before stopping to relieve himself. As he did, he grunted, "I'm ready to believe your mamas raised pure idiots."

"I ain't no idiot," Cooney shot back.

"Me, neither," Hank quickly agreed.

"What'cha mean by saying that, anyhow?" Cooney wanted to know.

"Yeah," Hank agreed, suddenly finding some backbone. "Me and Cooney don't 'preciate being branded idiots." He kicked a patch of greasewood.

"Simmer down, simmer down," Fargo began. "What else can I think? In one day you two got caught red-handed by a female, and Hank just tried to outrun a bullet. She got the drop on you way out in the wide open spaces. It would have been different if she had tracked you in boulders or forests, but, no, you didn't even see or hear her coming."

"We was counting," Hank mumbled.

Fargo started buttoning up. "You two look like decent sorts. Stupid, but decent. What prompted you to start robbing?"

Cooney answered while Fargo marched them back to the mesquite. " 'Cause we were out of work and flat broke."

"That's no reason," Fargo replied.

Hank said, "We reckoned we'd try our luck in California."

"Now that's a reason, pitiful as it is," Fargo answered. "I suggest you work your way out there next time, when you get out of jail."

"I ain't going to no jail," Cooney mumbled.

Nothing more was said until the camp fire blazed. Putting the coffeepot on to boil, Fargo asked Apache how much farther they had to ride before getting to Stockton. "We should see the camp within three days," she answered. "Why?"

"With an ounce of luck, we will find a woman to look after the girl."

"Don't count on it," Apache began. "Whites don't take in Apache children. Not out here, they don't. Wait and see, they won't even speak to me. And they have good reason not to. I could be scouting for a war party."

Hank and Cooney sat about ten feet from the fire, staring into it. Fargo and Pilar sat on the far side of it, looking up at Apache, who stood with her arms folded at her bosom.

"Are you?" Cooney muttered.

Turning to face him, Apache lowered her arms, but said nothing. Fargo saw her penetrating stare fix on Cooney's eyes. He wondered how she would handle the oblique accusation.

Cooney spat, "Indian bitch!"

Her left hand whipped her six-gun from its holster, and she shot off Cooney's right earlobe. Cooney yelped and grabbed his hanging ear. Holstering the Colt,

Apache took two strides going to her saddle. Reaching for her bullwhip, she said, "Cooney, you're lucky I didn't kill you." Uncoiling the whip, she continued, "Now, I'm going to hurt you many times. Fargo, please untie the sniveling bastard."

Fargo rose and stepped to him. Untying Cooney's wrists, he muttered, "You're a bigger idiot than I realized."

When Fargo stepped away, Cooney rubbed his wrists, then charged Apache with his arms spread wide.

She spun away gracefully, Cooney's fingers missing her by less than an inch. He stumbled and fell. Apache lashed his rump twice and ordered him to get up. "Take your punishment like a man," she thundered.

Cooney staggered to his feet and started running. Fargo watched the end of the bullwhip coil around Cooney's left ankle. Apache jerked back. Cooney toppled facedown in a bed of prickly pears. He screamed, not from the needles in his face, but from the blistering bullwhip on his back. Altogether Apache gave him twelve lashes. The back of Cooney's shirt was shredded. Red welts crisscrossed his bare skin. She looked at Hank.

Hank told her, "I didn't say anything, lady."

Apache coiled and returned the bullwhip to the pommel.

Fargo poured a canteen of water on Cooney's stripes, came back to the fire, and filled his tin cup with steaming brew. "Where were we?" he asked. He filled a cup with water and handed it to the girl.

"Discussing the Indian problem," she answered. "Prejudices run deep on both sides. I think it best I wait for you on the edge of Saint Gall. You can take these two to the guardhouse and try to make arrangements in Saint Gall for the girl."

"Saint Gall?"

"Yes. A small settlement near the camp. I'll wait for you on the other side of Saint Gall."

Fargo shook his head. Splitting up was tantamount to perpetuating the problem. He said, "No, you stay with me. Anybody in the army wants to make a fuss about it, they will have me to deal with."

"I fight my own fights, Fargo, and in my own way. I'll ride or walk the full mile with my partner, providing he doesn't take up for me. Agreed?"

"Agreed," Fargo answered.

He watched Apache go to Hank and untie his hands. "Get up and drag Cooney over here. Make your bedding ready. After eating, go to sleep."

Hank didn't give her any backchat. He got up and did what he was told.

Apache came back to the fire and fixed them a tin plate of jerky and pinto beans spiced with chiles. Fargo picked through his beans and isolated most of the fiery chiles that caused his lips to feel like they were curling. Pilar, he noticed, ate every one of hers.

Finished, Fargo wiped his and the girl's plates clean as he could, then relieved the Ovaro of his gear. He opened his bedroll next to the fire and winked at Pilar. She snuggled inside, looked at him, and smiled. "Don't flirt with me," Fargo told her. "I'm not the marrying type." He shot her another wink.

Hank and Cooney were bound for the night. Fargo noticed Cooney preferred sleeping on his belly. Fargo heard them whispering to each other, Cooney saying, "We'll make a break for it after they go to sleep."

The last thing Fargo did before retiring was to bind both clumsy robbers with his throwing rope and secure it to the Ovaro. "Boys, that's the smartest horse in the world," he told them. "If either of you take a strain on this rope . . . Well, I won't be responsible for what he does to you."

Hank looked at the rope and the stallion and stammered, "What do you mean by that?"

"No telling," Fargo muttered. "He goes crazy, though. He's been known to trample the source of the strain, other times he just starts running. Sleep well."

Fargo had another cup of coffee. Apache's bedroll lay out of the dim glow of the firelight. She was already inside it. Fargo pitched the coffee grounds on the embers, pulled off his boots, and got in with Pilar.

The girl was already asleep. He pulled her to him and drifted into sleep, staring into the embers of the fire.

The pinto nickering lowly snapped his eyes open. His hand gripped the Colt as he raised and checked on Hank and Cooney. Both lay facedown, snoring softly. He looked in Apache's direction.

In a hushed tone, he heard her say, "Ssst! Fargo! I need your help."

He pulled on his boots and went to check on her. Squatting next to her bedroll, he saw everything appeared all right. At first he thought what Winston and Garrison had said about her abstaining from sex was not so. He was wrong.

She whispered, "There's a rattlesnake in here with me."

"How do you know it's a rattler?" Fargo asked.

"I can feel its buttons on my left thigh."

"Are you naked?"

"Half. I kept my shirt on. This is so awkward. What am I to do?"

"First, don't panic or move a muscle."

"Don't worry. I'm too terrified to do either. Tell me what to do. I've never been in this kind of a fix before, and I'm . . . Oh, God, it's moving. Hurry and think of something. Please!"

Fargo scratched his jaw. "Is the snake on your left side?"

"No. I told you it moved. Now it's stretched across my, uh, bottom. Oh, God, it's big and heavy."

"Okay, where's the snake's head? Left or right?"

"I don't know, Fargo. Please, get it off me."

"Before I stick my hand in there, I have to know where the head is. We'll have to wait for it to move again."

"Wait? Wait? You don't know what you're asking. I want it out. Now!"

Fargo sat and rubbed his face. He glanced skyward. The Big Dipper was in its four-o'clock position. He considered grabbing Apache by the armpits and yanking her out of the bedroll. He rejected the idea. The rattler might come out on top of her. A new thought occurred to him. He said, "Don't move. I'll be back."

"Back? Where are you going? Don't leave me here like this."

Fargo went to his bedroll and felt under it. His hand grasped the Arkansas toothpick's handle. Returning to Apache, he showed her the stiletto and said, "I'll have to ruin your bedroll."

"Go ahead. It moved again while you were gone. It's coiled, I think on the small of my back."

"Here's what I'm going to do. I'll slice down the right side and pull the bedroll back, grab the snake behind the head, and pull it off you. Ready?"

Fargo positioned the stiletto and made the initial cut. Halfway down the bedroll the blade nipped Apache's hip. She flinched, then screamed. Fargo instantly let go of the stiletto and jerked her out of the bedroll.

Apache grabbed for the back of her right shoulder, saying, "It bit me."

Hank and Cooney sat up. Hank said, "Hey, you two, stop screwing so loud. I'm trying to sleep."

Fargo pulled her shirt off, felt over the shoulder, and found a small lump. "The rattler tagged you all right. I can feel where the fangs entered." He picked up the stiletto and cut an X over the swelling, then started sucking and spitting the venom out. "I think I got most of it," he said. "Time will tell."

Apache was more concerned over his seeing her nakedness. Turning her back to him, she bent and picked up her pants. He watched her shapely fanny disappear inside the trousers. The big rattler slithered from the bedding and quickly vanished. "I'll build a fire," Fargo told her, "then take a look at that shoulder."

Cooney, aware that something other than sex had been going on, asked, "What happened? Why all the racket?"

Breaking dead limbs off the mesquite, Fargo answered, "A diamondback bit Apache."

Cooney and Hank exchanged smiles. Fargo heard Cooney mutter, "Good, I hope she dies."

"Cooney boy, I heard that," Fargo said. "You better hope and pray she doesn't, because if she does, I won't hesitate to shoot both of you assholes. Killing the likes of you will make my job easier and faster."

Fargo soon had a fire blazing. Apache sat next to it and bared her right shoulder for him. Though he wasn't sure, he said, "I see the fang mark. Where I cut there may be others. It's swollen to beat hell, and dark red. Does it hurt too bad?"

"Stings a little," she answered.

"Leave the shoulder exposed till sunup. The wound needs to dry."

She looked over her shoulder at him and said, "Thank you, Fargo, for trying." She turned a little farther, leaned into his arms, kissed him, and whispered, "That's your reward. It's the best I can offer."

"I know, I know," he mumbled, but the nipple punching his muscled right biceps promised more. Much more.

Apache remained in his embrace until shortly before sunrise, at which time they had to disengage to make the horses and mule ready for the trail. Saddling Hank's horse, he watched Apache make Lulu ready. She seemed to waiver, as though undecided about what to do next. He asked, "Apache, are you all right?"

Nodding, she answered, "Yes, a little dizzy, but it will pass."

He finished with Hank's horse and moved to his own. Ten minutes later they headed south. He asked her, "You sure you feel all right?"

"I'm fine, Fargo, really I am. Don't worry about me." She pulled her neckerchief over her nose and mumbled, "I've never felt so vulnerable as I do now." Looking at him, she added, "What's happening to me, Fargo?"

He didn't know if her feeling was due to the snakebite or the exposure of her nakedness to him, the quick kiss. Surely she had felt her nipple resting against his upper arm. If what Garrison and Winston said was true, then the rubbing had to arouse her dormant desires. On the other hand, a snakebite, especially a poisonous one, always brought on shock. He said, "The shock is just now catching up with you. That's what's happening. It will pass."

But it didn't. By sundown, when Fargo reined the Ovaro to a halt, Apache was sweating profusely, shaking from head to foot. He dismounted and had to help her from her saddle. She leaned against El Negro while he spread her bedroll, then she collapsed onto it. He felt her forehead and said, "You're ice-cold, Apache."

"Don't leave me," she murmured.

"Hey! What about us?" Cooney cried. "We're hungry."

"Shut up," Fargo bellowed. "I'll take care of you later." He lifted Pilar off the saddle and told her to get inside Apache's bedroll and snuggle up to her. Then he made a fire. When he went to Lulu to fetch a canteen of water to brew coffee, he found all but four empty. He took one containing water to Apache. She refused it. He had to force her to drink. He divided the remainder between the horses and mule, came back, knelt beside Apache, and said, "We need water. Think you'll be all right long enough for me to go search for some?"

"Don't leave me," she repeated.

The slur in her voice told him she was slipping into unconsciousness fast. He felt her forehead again. She was burning up with fever. He decided to wait until it broke. He ordered Hank and Cooney to dismount and sit by the fire. He fed them and Pilar beans, himself and Apache nothing. Fargo checked her fever frequently. The unconscious woman seemed to be getting hotter. He told Pilar to come out, then opened the bedroll and drained a canteen on Apache's head and down her body. He unbuttoned her shirt, rolled her limp body over, and looked at the snakebite. It was infected. Pouring another canteen of water on the inflamed area, he decided not to wait for the fever to break. Apache desperately needed water. He instructed Pilar to stay with her, then handed her the last canteen of water and told the girl, "Give Apache all the water she wants when she wakes up. *Comprendes*?"

The girl nodded.

Fargo ordered Hank and Cooney to mount up; he was taking them to find water. Grumbling, they obeyed.

He rode east at a gallop. Shortly after midnight dark clouds raced overhead and blotted out the stars. Half an hour later, it began to drizzle. The strong odor of creosote was immediate. He pushed on and, after about an hour more, came to a stream. He dismounted in the middle of it and began filling the canteens while the thirsty horses and mule watered. Pulling Hank and Cooney from their saddles, he told them, "Boys, this is your last change to bathe before going to jail. Make it snappy." He fell facedown in the stream.

The drizzle gave way to a downpour on their way back, making it impossible for Fargo to follow their outbound tracks. He relied on his sixth sense of dead reckoning to show him the way.

He proceeded a short distance farther, then dismounted and searched on foot for El Negro. Now and then he paused and felt over the wet ground to maybe find their hoofprints.

Cooney called to him, "She's gone, big man."

When Fargo turned to tell him to shut his mouth, Hank nodded toward her empty bedroll.

# 9

Fargo climbed into his saddle and stared through the falling rain, deep in thought. First he considered the worst: Apache, Pilar, and El Negro had wandered off one at a time in different directions. But he didn't put much stock in that thought. No, they had left together. The cool rainwater had probably brought Apache out of her delirium long enough to get in the saddle. He could imagine her sitting there confused. Left to itself, the gelding would instinctively put its rump to the wind and rain. The rain tonight blew from the north-northwest. Fargo decided a southerly course would be as good as any, so he turned and headed in that direction. At dawn maybe he would spot El Negro.

For once he was glad for the flat landscape. Figuring the gelding moved at a walk, he walked the black-and-white. Not knowing when Apache left, he didn't want to pass her during the night. It was possible. He'd missed spotting the bedroll, and he was damn near standing on it. Cooney and Hank had made another mistake by drawing his attention to it. If he'd gone a few paces farther, he'd have missed it completely. He rewarded their observation. "Boys, if you hadn't said anything about that bedroll till later, I'd have probably shot you dead."

Neither man replied.

Dawn broke to an overcast sky. The rain had slackened to a misty drizzle. Fargo couldn't see the horizon. Visibility was less than an eighth of a mile. He watched the ground, occasionally scanning left and right through the mist.

At midmorning the hot sun burned off the clouds

enough to cause the mist to stop falling. Visibility lengthened, though he still couldn't see the horizon. Doggedly, he pressed on, wondering if El Negro had halted and he'd passed Apache during the night. He wondered how much farther it was to Camp Stockton. He wondered about a lot of things. In the end he told himself that after dropping off Hank and Cooney, he'd come back and find her and Pilar.

By noon the trailing edge of the thin clouds passed overhead and the sun appeared. Then began the sweltering heat. He was watching the ground when in his peripheral vision he saw the stallion's ears perk and swivel left. Fargo glanced east, then squinted. El Negro was about a mile away, walking among dead mesquites.

He reined left and nudged the Ovaro into a gallop to make the intercept.

Coming closer, he saw Apache slumped over the gelding's neck, Pilar riding behind her. The girl waved when she saw him. Fargo rode up alongside the gelding, dismounted, and halted the horse. He lifted Apache from the saddle and laid her on her left side on the ground.

Hank and Cooney watched as he started breaking mesquite at the base. Hank asked, "What'cha doing that for? Seems to me the littler pieces would be better for making a fire. Hank?"

Fargo didn't answer. Soon he had a tidy stack of mesquite trunks. He stepped to Lulu and got a canvas bag filled with shorter lengths of rope that she planned to use to tie up the Scoggins gang.

Hank and Cooney leaned on their saddle horns while watching a travois take shape.

"What's he making?" Hank wondered aloud.

"Your guess is as good as mine," Cooney answered. "But it damn sure ain't no fire."

Finished, Fargo hitched the travois to Lulu, then spread his bedroll over the lattice. He laid Apache on it and stepped to Cooney's horse and began removing the man's bedroll.

Cooney whined, "What'cha getting my bedroll for?"

"To cover her, you asshole," Fargo hissed.

"Oh, no, you ain't," Cooney protested. "Ain't no Injun whore's stink gonna get on my—"

Fargo's hard backhand blow to Cooney's mouth clipped short his complaint.

The big man trailed Lulu to El Negro. Handing Pilar the hackamore reins, he said, "Think you're big enough to handle this big horse?" She nodded and he shot her a grin with a wink.

He checked the throwing rope holding Apache in place one more time, then mounted up and headed south.

Apache stirred out of her stupor during the night. Fargo lay by the fire, his horse blanket for bedding and his saddle for a pillow. Her soft moan opened his eyes instantly. Shoving back his hat, he glanced at her and Pilar. "Apache," he muttered, "are you awake?"

He watched her eyelids flutter open. He knelt beside her, brushed a strand of hair from her face.

She murmured, "I'm so thirsty."

He went and got a canteen, held it to her waiting lips. "Just a sip or two at first," he cautioned.

She started to rise, but collapsed. After a moment she looked at him and said, "Fargo, I feel as though I ran a hard footrace and lost. I'm terribly weak. Where are we?"

"Close to the camp," he answered hopefully. "Should be there tomorrow. By the way, you won that footrace. Hungry?"

"Starving."

"We have beans and jerky or jerky and beans. Or, if you prefer, I'll chase down a rabbit."

She opted for the beans and jerky. He fixed a plate for her. She mustered up the strength to sit. Drawing up her knees, she rested her chin on them, looked at Pilar, and asked, "When did she start bunking with me and not you?"

"Pilar? She's been your constant companion since the onset of your fever and your delirium." He handed her the plate of trail food. "Don't you remember putting her on the saddle behind you?"

"No."

"Well, you did." He went on to tell her about leaving the girl to look after her while he searched for water, the deluge, and coming back and finding the two of them gone. "You and I owe that little girl a lot," he concluded.

"I'll make it up to her, buy her a new dress. God knows she's been wearing that one fashioned out of burlap long enough. I'm tired, Fargo. Real tired."

"I imagine so. Riding on a travois can be rough going."

"Travois? I've seen them, but haven't ever ridden on one."

"You have now. Put your back to me. I want to see your wound."

She turned her back to the fire and slipped her shirt off the right shoulder. "It's sore," she told him.

He saw the swelling had gone down a tad, and the cut marks he'd made had crusted over. "We'll have the camp's doctor look at it tomorrow, clean it out. Finished with those beans?" He tugged her shirt back in place.

Handing him the empty plate, she allowed, "How bad is it?"

"Lousy. Your shoulder looks like it has been in a dogfight and lost."

He watched her shrug the shoulder a couple of times. "Good thing I draw from the left."

"I thought you brought them back alive," he teased.

"I do," she mocked. "But first I have to get their attention."

"Have you been up against a gang before?"

She shook her head, "Not really. I faced three. Had to kill one."

"Scoggins might be different than anything you've ever seen. He and his men and sister are ruthless people. The stories you've heard about them are half-stories, isolated incidents. I've fought men like them. They don't give a damn if they live or die. What I'm saying, Apache, is it won't be easy. You will have to be up to full strength for this fight. You need all the rest you can get, time for the snakebite to completely heal."

"How much time?"

"At least a week, maybe longer."

He watched her slip back inside his bedroll, then cuddle the girl in her arms. Looking at him, she smiled and said, "We don't have a week, Fargo. You know that."

The Trailsman reclined, pulled his hat down over his eyes, and went to sleep thinking of forests, waterfalls, canyons, and pretty meadows. It all seemed so far away. He wondered if he would ever see any of it again.

Fargo's eyes snapped open at first light. He sensed the presence of somebody, someone watching him from close range. His gun hand moved slowly beneath the saddle-pillow and gripped the Colt's handle. At the same time he tilted his head back and peered past the brim of his hat.

Pilar sat facing him, her coal-black eyes a study of concentration on his. The neckerchief was pulled up just below her eyes. He lifted the edge of the neckerchief and saw a winsome smile. Picking her up, he sat her astride his abdomen and whispered, "You're heavy, *niña*. Good morning."

"Uncle Fargo," she began, "can I ride on that stick thing you made for Aunt Isabel?"

"Uncle Fargo? Aunt Isabel? And where, may I ask, did you hear that?" He couldn't recall her using either reference until now.

Pilar pointed behind and said, "Back there when Aunt Isabel was *loca*. She told me your name. She told me not to call her Apache. She told me to call her Aunt Isabel."

Through a soft chuckle he said, "Well, *niña*, if Aunt Isabel is strong enough to get in the saddle, I suppose it will be all right for you to ride on the stick thing. You'll have to hang on, though. It's rather bumpy."

Pilar raised the neckerchief, bent, and kissed his cheek. "I love you, Uncle Fargo," she whispered.

"What's this?" Apache spoke sleepily. "Did I hear love?"

" 'Morning, Aunt Isabel." He chuckled. "Pilar just asked if she could take your place on the travois. I told her she could if you were strong enough to ride."

"I'll ride in my saddle, thank you. Now, you're going to explain the Aunt Isabel remark."

Shrugging, Fargo replied, "That's what you said for her to call you. At the time you were *loca*. Her words, not mine." He sat Pilar beside Apache and got up. Facing east, he said, "We'll wait and have a late breakfast of bacon and eggs at Camp Stockton." Strengthening his voice, he told Hank and Cooney to wake up, he was breaking camp.

A spectacular sunrise caught the five riders—Pilar on the travois—moving among yucca. In the far distance Fargo saw the hazy blue outline of mountaintops peeking over the horizon. He glanced at Apache.

She said, "A few more miles and the camp should come into view."

"How is the shoulder feeling?"

"Fine."

He dropped back to the travois and asked, "Rough ride, *niña*?"

"It's fun, Uncle Fargo. I get to see where we've been."

"Riders coming in," Apache called back to him.

Fargo pulled up alongside her and looked where she pointed. A group of riders, mere specks on the flat land, came toward them. As they came closer, he saw they were army troopers, four in all. Closer still, they swung right, spread out, and rode a safe distance parallel to Fargo's group. He surmised they were sizing them up before approaching any closer. He was correct.

Finally the troopers closed ranks and rode up to them. Fargo saw the sergeant's stripes and presumed he led the patrol. The sergeant's eyes moved from the travois to Apache, his men's from Hank and Cooney to Fargo and back.

"Where you headed, stranger?" the sergeant asked, a trace of Irish in his voice.

"Is there a doctor in Camp Stockton?" Fargo answered their question with one of his own.

The lanky sergeant spit a brown stream of tobacco juice before replying, "Of course. Doc White. What do you need him for?" He glanced at Pilar, and added, "The Injin kid?"

Nodding toward Apache, Fargo told him, "No. The lady got bit by a rattler."

"Did she, now?" the sergeant said, a hint of sarcasm in the tone. He nodded toward Hank and Cooney and asked, "Why you got them tied up?"

"They robbed a Butterfield stage back in Crescent Gap. My partner chased them down and made the capture."

"Carl Stadum mentioned getting robbed." Fargo saw another brown stream spurt through the Irishman's bushy mustache. The sergeant asked, "Where is your partner? I want to shake his hand."

Apache extended hers.

Fargo looked at the sergeant's puzzled expression and said through an easy grin, "Go ahead and take it, Sergeant. She doesn't have anything catching."

The sergeant's facial muscles tightened as he reluctantly grasped Apache's hand and shook it once.

In perfect English, Apache said, "Why, thank you, Sergeant. My name is Isabel Sayas. And you are . . . ?"

He cleared his throat, then grunted, "Sergeant Jeremy Donahue."

"How far to Stockton?" Fargo asked.

"About five miles," Donahue answered. "Seen any Comanche?"

"Not between here and Crescent Gap," Fargo offered. "But we saw what they did at Río Pecos." He went on to relate what they found at both Rancho de Sueño and the village.

"When you get to Camp Stockton, mention what you just told me to Major Benton. He'll be interested. Gotta go now. Damn Apaches raided the Slidell spread. Rufe's mad as tarnation over losing steers to 'em." He touched the brim of his hat, told his men to break off. "They're all right," Fargo heard him tell them.

Sure enough, after going less than five miles Camp Stockton came into view. Soon they arrived on the outskirts of St. Gall and bypassed the little settlement for the camp. Fargo asked a soldier where to find headquarters and the major. Pointing to an adobe structure, the soldier told him, "That's where you will find Major Benton."

Fargo led his little group to the building, halted, and dismounted. "Wait here and keep your eyes on the boys," he said, "while I have a chat with Benton."

A young soldier guarding the front entrance nodded when Fargo stepped inside. Although every window and door was wide open, the room felt stuffy to Fargo. A stocky sergeant sat behind a desk. He looked up from his paperwork when Fargo entered.

The Trailsman told him, "My name's Skye Fargo and—"

The sergeant's beaming smile cut short Fargo's intended statement. Rising, the sergeant said, "I heard about you. Carl Stadum spoke highly of you." He came around the desk and stuck out his hand. "You still got those two men?"

Shaking hands with him, Fargo said, "Yes. They're outside. That's what I want to talk to the major about."

The burly man stepped to the door to see for himself. "They don't look like much," he grunted. Coming back to the desk, he said, "Major Benton has Rufe Slidell in his office. They're jawboning about the Indian menace. Rufe lost a dozen longhorns to them."

"I heard," Fargo mentioned.

"How? Where?" the sergeant wondered aloud.

"Sergeant Donahue met us coming in."

But the man only half-heard him. He was focused on a large green-blue fly walking across his desk. Fargo watched the sergeant's open hand shoot out and close around the fly. When he opened the hand, they both looked. The fly wasn't in it. "Damn," the sergeant grunted. "Missed again." Returning his attention to Fargo, he asked, "What were you saying? Something about Donahue?"

"That's right. We met him about five miles out."

"What's your business with the major? I have to ask."

Fargo told about the massacres, but not about Apache's needing a doctor. "Donahue said I should report the massacre to Major Benton."

"I'm sure he would want to hear firsthand."

Fargo watched him step inside the adjoining room. In a few seconds the major appeared in the doorway and motioned Fargo in. The major's face showed signs of tiredness. When he spoke, his voice did also. "Sergeant Babcock, here, says you want to report massacres. Apache or Comanche?" He moved behind his desk and sat.

Fargo looked at Rufe Slidell, an older man bronzed by the sun. They exchanged nods. Major Benton said, "Have a seat—Fargo, isn't it?"

This room was hotter than the first. Sunlight spilled through the only window. Pulling a straight-back out of the sunlight, Fargo nodded and began the report. At the conclusion of it, he added, "My partner has two prisoners she plans to take back—"

That's as far as Fargo got. Major Benton leaned forward and whispered in a disturbing tone, "She? She?" He glanced questioningly to Sergeant Babcock. "You didn't tell me about a woman."

Babcock stiffened, cleared his throat, and replied, "She is guarding them out front."

Benton came around his desk immediately. Fargo and Rufe followed him as far as the front door. Benton took a spread-feet, hands-on-hips stance and surveyed the tall woman astride the black horse. Isabel glanced at him and nodded. Twisting to face those in the doorway, the major snorted, "She's Mexican!"

Isabel set the record straight. "Apache. Jicarilla."

"My God, what next?" Major Benton mumbled. He looked at Pilar, then swiftly cut his gaze onto Hank and Cooney, who sat glum-faced in their saddles. Benton wheeled, strode past Fargo and Slidell, headed for his office.

When Fargo and Rufe came into the office, the major was pouring himself a stiff drink of whiskey.

Fargo said, "As I was saying, Major, she plans to take those two, and God only knows how many more, back to Austin for trial."

"What did you say?" Benton sputtered. "There's others?"

"The Scoggins gang," Fargo answered.

Slidell and Major Benton shared a laugh. Slidell said, "Scoggins will feed her to the wolves."

Benton added, sourly, "Disgusting thought."

Their attitude was wearing thin on Fargo. He said evenly, "Major, we need to keep this pair in your guardhouse till we round up Scoggins."

Benton looked at him over the rim of his glass. Sitting, he sighed and finally replied, "Mr. Fargo, I suggest you abandon this folly and return to Austin immediately. I've been trying to catch Scoggins ever since I assumed command of this camp, and I've failed."

Slidell hurried to add, "What makes you think you and the woman can succeed, when the U.S. Army could not? Please, enlighten us."

Fargo answered, "The army can't cross the border." He glanced at Benton and asked, "True?"

Benton replied, "We know they run to Boquillas. I have men watching the village. So far, Scoggins has eluded them. But, Mr. Fargo, it's only a matter of time before we catch the bastards. Again, I say give up your pursuit. The army will take care of the problem."

Slidell gave credence to Fargo's quest, saying, "Like the army is taking care of the Indian problem, Major?"

Fargo jumped into the breach. "Major, the Comanche are on the move. You're going to need every man you can muster to handle them, those watching the village included. Put these two in your guardhouse so we can be on our way."

Benton stepped to the window and looked out. After a long moment he shouted for Sergeant Babcock. Babcock appeared in the doorway, said, "Sir?"

Without turning Benton asked, "Sergeant, how many prisoners are in the guardhouse?"

"I don't know, sir."

"Goddammit, then find out."

"Yes, sir."

When the sergeant retreated, Benton went back to his desk, poured another drink, and said, "Our guardhouse has limited space. Pitiful and inadequate at best." He looked at Rufe and justified, "Mr. Slidell, we're doing the best we can to protect you people from marauding Indians. We have a lot of territory to cover, and frankly, I don't have enough men to cover all of it properly."

Picking up a sheet of paper, he continued. "The truth is, we might be pulling out altogether. I received this communiqué in the mail brought by the last Butterfield stage. In a nutshell, it tells me to be prepared to abandon Camp Stockton. I don't know, gentlemen, but I suspect war is closer than any of us realize."

Slidell shot to his feet. "Pulling out? Pulling out?" he half-shouted. "You'd leave us to the mercy of those savages?"

"Calm down, Mr. Slidell," the major began, speaking in a tired voice. "The communiqué simply advises me to stay in a state of readiness . . . just in case."

Slidell collapsed in his chair.

Benton tossed down a slug of whiskey.

Fargo said, "You have a doctor?"

Benton grunted, "Yes. Captain White. Why?"

"My partner got bit by a rattler. I want him to take a look at the bite."

Thoroughly exasperated, Benton rested his elbows on the desk, put his face in his hands, and shook his head slowly, saying, "What next, Mr. Fargo?"

Fargo reached for the bottle of whiskey. After swilling from it, he said dryly, "I need somebody to take care of the girl while we're away."

Benton peered between his fingers at Fargo. A low chuckle rose out of his throat, after which he said, "You come in my office, ask me to take two prisoners off your hands, tell me that you're going to add the whole Scoggins gang shortly, ask me to provide a doctor for a snakebite, then have the gall to say you want me to take care of a small child. Really, Mr. Fargo, you are the most wanting person I've ever met. To top it all off, you help yourself to my whiskey. I'm a busy man, Mr. Fargo."

The sergeant's reappearance saved Benton from a tongue-lashing by Fargo. The haggard man simply didn't understand Fargo's situation. The sergeant reported, "Sir, there are six prisoners in the guardhouse, two in the holding cell, and two in solitary confinement."

Benton sighed and said, "All right, Sergeant, you're dismissed. No! Wait. Get Captain White over here."

"That all, Major?" Babcock asked.

"For the time being." Shifting attention back to Fargo, Benton said, "The guardhouse is overcrowded. I can't accept your prisoners."

Fargo turned to Rufe Slidell and said, "My apologies, Mr. Slidell, but I must ask you to step out of the room. There is something I have to tell Major Benton in private."

"I was about to leave, anyhow," Slidell grunted. He rose, shook Fargo's hand, and offered, "Good luck, Mr. Fargo. With the Scoggins gang and the U.S. Army." Going through the doorway, he added, "You'll need it with both."

Fargo closed the door and stepped to Benton's desk. "Major, Apache and I are on a secret mission for the Governor of Texas." Benton's eyes kicked up to Fargo's. "That's right, Major, I said the governor. I understand your problem. While I can't relieve it in regard to the Indian menace, I can and intend to bring an end to the Scoggins menace. You're hindering my progress by refusing our captives. The governor isn't going to take kindly to that when he hears about it. I suggest you make room in your guardhouse for our prisoners, even if it means turning loose two of yours. Do I make myself clear?"

"Clear as a church bell," Benton muttered. Fargo watched him return to the window, where he said, "I'm tired, Mr. Fargo, dog-tired from chasing phantoms. My men, God bless them, try their best, but they are tired also. Between this blasted heat and the

Indians in this godforsaken hellhole they call Big Bend, tempers and good common sense wear out fast." He paused to face Fargo, then continued. "Frankly, Mr. Fargo, I don't want . . . No, I don't need the governor adding to my problems. One letter of complaint from him to my superiors is all it would take for the army to call me and my men to the rear. I don't want that to happen. How long do you think I would have to accommodate your prisoners?"

"As long as it takes us to go to Boquillas and back."

"Five days. Say, about a week. I suppose I can release Privates Foster and McRae early. They're in the guardhouse for drunk and disorderly conduct. Yes, I can take your prisoners."

"What about the girl?"

"Not even a letter from the governor could cause the army to make me do that, Mr. Fargo. If the child were a little boy, maybe I could bend the rules, but not for a girl. I'm sorry, but you will have to look elsewhere. I don't want the responsibility."

"Maybe I can find a woman in Saint Gall to look after her."

"Perhaps," Benton replied, "but I wouldn't count on it happening. If she were a white . . ."

Fargo nodded. Moving to the door, he opened it. The breeze was immediate and refreshing. A young captain sat waiting in the outer office. When Fargo gestured for him to come into Benton's office, he stood and came smiling. Fargo liked him at once, and returned his smile. "Hello, Captain," he said, extending his hand. He liked the captain's firm grip, too.

Benton said, "You saw the tall female outside. She was bitten by a rattlesnake. Fargo, here, wants you to inspect the wound. Uh, where, exactly, did the rattlesnake bite her?"

"Three days north of here." Fargo grinned. When the two officers chuckled, Fargo explained, "On the right shoulder." He glanced at Captain White and said, "Don't get your hopes up. The snakebite is on her back."

123

"Just my luck," White replied. "I haven't touched a woman in six months."

Benton called the sergeant into his office and told him, "Take Mr. Fargo's prisoners to the guardhouse and lock them up. Tell whoever is on duty I said so. I know, I know, Sergeant, there's not enough room for two additional guests. I'll sign the order to release Foster and McRae first thing in the morning." A wave of his hand dismissed Babcock. Benton looked at Fargo and asked, "Anything else?"

Fargo shook his head.

"Then leave me to cope with more-pressing matters." Benton bent to the paperwork on his desk.

Fargo led Captain White outside to Apache. "Hear you got bit by a rattler, ma'am," White began. "Get off that pretty horse and follow me."

Apache dismounted haltingly, as though something bothered her. She looked nervously at Pilar perched on the travois. Her body language clearly conveyed to Fargo that she didn't want to be alone with White.

Fargo suggested, "Take the girl with you. I've got other business to tend to." He shot her a wink.

Apache called the girl to her.

"I'm going to Saint Gall to make arrangements for her," Fargo explained. "Captain, is there a shady place where they can wait after you're finished?"

Apache answered, "You will find me under a tree by the springs."

"Good choice," White commented. "Ma'am?" He gestured for her to follow him.

Fargo released the trailing rope holding Hank's and Cooney's horses and hitched them to the rail outside Benton's headquarters. Mounting up, he saw Babcock coming back and asked if he would arrange to have the two horses stabled for about a week, "until we bring in the Scoggins gang."

"Sure thing, Mr. Fargo. What about the gelding and mule?"

"No, she will come for them after White does his work." He turned the Ovaro and rode off the parade grounds.

In St. Gall, he stopped at the first house he came to. A man was chopping firewood out back. Fargo rode to him and introduced himself. "I see children's clothes hanging on the line," Fargo began. "I was wondering if you and your wife could look after a four-year-old girl for about a week. I can pay."

"How much?" the fellow asked between swings of his ax.

"Ten dollars sound fair?"

The man squinted up at him and shouted, "Mavis! Mavis! Come out here!" Holding the squint, he told Fargo, "Ten dollars is a heap of money, stranger. What did you say your name was?"

"Fargo. Skye Fargo."

A skinny woman, full-bellied with child, came outside. Looking at Fargo, she whined to her husband, "What'cha want me for, Pete?"

"Man wants to know if we can take care of his kid for a week. He can pay ten dollars. Think you're up to it? That's a lot of cash."

Fargo hastened to say, "She's not my child. Her mother was killed by Comanche. Mexican-Apache mother, I might add."

"Ain't interested," Pete replied without giving the mother any further thought.

Mavis went back in the house.

Fargo rode to the next house, where he made the same offer and received a similar rejection.

After visiting four more homes and getting turned away quickly, he moseyed back to Camp Stockton. He saw El Negro and Lulu standing in a grove of elm trees and went to them. Apache and Pilar sat in shade near the spring. Questioningly, he asked, "What did Doc White have to say?"

"He cleaned it with alcohol, then smeared ointment over it and told me to keep the bandage on till morning. He's a nice man, gentle. Did you have any luck?"

Reclining on a wide patch of grass, he told her, "No. The last place I tried, I offered twenty dollars, but they said, 'Not for any amount.' So, I quit asking."

"The big sergeant?"

"Babcock?"

"He saw me getting on El Negro and came out. He said to tell you that Hank and Cooney intend to register a complaint about throwing them in a jail built for three rather than six. They have to sleep on the floor."

"Tough luck. Speaking of sleep, have you picked out a spot for us? I'll talk Major Benton into feeding us army grub for a change, now that I know that a letter from the governor works."

"You didn't?" she said through a grin.

"Oh, yes, I did." He told her about using it as leverage to get him to take Hank and Cooney.

"You're a scoundrel, Fargo, but I like your style. Why not spend the night right here?"

"Fine with me. We can leave at daybreak, get a jump on the heat. Major Benton says it's a two and a half days' ride to the border."

"Sounds right. It took me four days to walk it."

"Weren't you scared? Alone, I mean."

"Not for one minute. You might say I was determined, much like now."

Fargo let it go at that. He got up, relieved Lulu of her burden, unsaddled both horses, and pitched his bedroll on the ground. "Plumb forgot you don't have a bedroll," he muttered. "I'll borrow one from the U.S. Army when I talk to Benton about feeding us."

Nodding, she changed the subject. "Fargo, I've never before brought back anyone from this distance, certainly no nine prisoners. I've been thinking about it. There's no way Lulu can haul that much food and water. Why don't you use that letter to borrow two more mules and about two dozen army canteens."

He chuckled. "You're forgetting their treasure. That will require a fourth mule. Why not one mule to tote the treasure, then leave the other problem lying dead in the street?" When, grim-jawed, she gave him a penetrating stare, he added, "In all probability that will happen if you like it or not. Isabel Sayas, you know I'm right."

She blinked, shook her head, as though clearing it, and said, "We've been together too long."

"What's that?"

"You called me by my real name. Isabel Sayas."

Now he blinked. "I'll go see about supper and the other things on your list."

He ambled across the parade grounds and went inside Benton's headquarters. Sergeant Babcock opened his hand and mumbled, "Missed again."

"Still trying to murder that fly?" Fargo mused aloud. The fly buzzed past Fargo's face. He and Babcock watched it enter dust-filled sunlight beams through the doorway, then circle back toward them. Fargo's gun hand shot out and closed. He held the hand close to his ear. Babcock leaned in. Fargo whispered, "He's in there, all right. Do I let him loose?"

"No," Babcock cried. "Kill the little son of a bitch."

Fargo opened his hand. The fly flew out. Fargo said, "I want to borrow three of your best mules and two dozen canteens. I'll pick up the food supplies in the morning. What's for supper?"

"The hell you say." In a loud voice, he said out of the corner of his mouth, "Major Benton, he's back, just like you said."

Benton stepped into the room. "What is it now, Mr. Fargo?"

"Mules, canteens, a bedroll, and supper, sir," Babcock answered.

"I can't spare any mules or canteens," Benton said. "I can have Sergeant Babcock tell the cook to feed you and see that you borrow a bedroll."

Fargo didn't bother testing his luck. Two out of four was better than none. He doubted the mules and canteens would be needed, anyhow. Fargo didn't intend for either Apache or him to go to boot hill. Nonetheless, he grimaced and nodded.

Benton inquired, "White fix up the woman with you?"

Fargo nodded.

Benton turned to Babcock and told him to see to Fargo's last two requests.

Fargo thanked him and left. In the doorway, he paused to turn and ask, "Sergeant, where's the guard-house? I want to check on my prisoners."

Babcock came to the doorway and pointed. "Keller's on duty. Tell him I said it was okay to let you in."

A lowering sun cast lengthening shadows across the parade grounds as Fargo crossed to the guardhouse. When he entered the adobe building, a young corporal sat behind a small desk, his feet atop it. Fargo said, "Sergeant Babcock said it was okay for me to check on my prisoners."

The young man didn't say a word as he unlocked a door and led Fargo to a long row of bars, then he said, "Take all the time you want. They aren't going nowhere." He turned and left, locking the door behind him.

Hank and two soldiers sat on a cot, two others on the one facing it from across the cell. Cooney stood at the barred window. All wore sullen expressions on their faces. Fargo could care less about their discomfort. He wasn't there to look in on the two wranglers gone bad, but to see for himself the soundness of the building, especially the cell. Fargo knew two-foot-thick adobe walls could be penetrated. He'd gone through one in the Tucson jail. It had taken him three days. Who was to say Hank's and Cooney's coprisoners were only inches away from effecting a breakout? Without entering the cell to make a close inspection, Fargo inspected its interior for signs of an escape. He saw none.

Fargo rapped on the connecting door. When the rawboned corporal unlocked it, Fargo looked at Cooney and said, "You and Hank better not give these people any trouble. I've left standing orders for them to throw your asses in solitary if you do," he lied. It would give them something to think about while he was away.

The heavy door grated open. Passing through the opening, Fargo muttered, "I'll come for them in a few days." Outside, he walked around the building and checked its exterior. Again he saw no evidence of an imminent breakout. As he passed the window, Cooney gripped the bars and pressed his face between two. Fargo paused and looked at him.

Cooney whispered, "I'll get out, big man, I'll get out. When I do—"

Whispering back, Fargo interrupted, "You'll be killed." He resumed his survey of the exterior.

Finished at the guardhouse, he went to the chow hall. It was easy enough to find. All he had to do was follow his nose. A long line of soldiers had formed at the entrance. Fargo went to the back door and stepped inside the kitchen. Aproned cooks were busy making last-minute preparations. The aroma of bread fresh out of the oven mingled with that of fried chicken.

A fat cook, sweating profusely, noticed him and asked, "You the one Babcock told me to feed?" He wiped his greasy hands on his apron as he came to Fargo.

Fargo nodded, saying, "There's two of us and a small child."

"Seen 'em down by the springs," he said. "Wait a minute and I'll bundle it up. Babcock left a bedroll here. It's inside, next to the door."

Fargo reached in and got the bedroll, watched him wrap several pieces of chicken in a cloth and bread in another, then put gravy and mashed spuds in bowls and bring all to him. "You can leave the empty bowls by the door. I'll find 'em at breakfast," the cook said.

"Thanks," Fargo replied. "Smells good."

"The old man insists," the cook explained. "We try." He shot Fargo a wink and bellowed to his helpers, "All right, you guys, let them hungry army men in."

Back at their campsite, Fargo set the food on the patch of grass, dropped the bedroll beside it.

Apache asked, "The mules and canteens?"

"I used up all my luck getting what you see. Sorry."

Opening the cloth containing the fried chicken, she allowed, "We'll make do with what we have. It's a lot better than I could have done. Major Benton will change his mind and give the rest to us when he sees Scoggins." She handed Pilar a drumstick.

They had eaten trail meals for so long that the home-cooked food satisfied their appetites quickly.

Half of the chicken was left untouched. Apache packed it in the cloth, saying, "For the trail tomorrow."

His belly full of vittles, Fargo opened the army bedroll and lay down. He alternately watched the sun sink below the horizon and the little girl at play, throwing pebbles in the spring nearby. Without intending, he drifted into sleep.

Hours later, a break in the camp's rhythm snapped his eyes open. Colt in hand, and cocked, he glanced at Apache in the army bedroll with the girl. Both were sound asleep. He listened, but heard nothing unusual. Two horses in the corral exchanged nickers, and that was it. He glanced heavenward. The Big Dipper was in the two-thirty position. Fully awake and needing to empty his bladder, Fargo got up. The gravy and mashed potato bowls lay empty on the grass. He picked them up and went to the kitchen door. After returning the bowls Fargo moved to the corner of the building, unbuttoned his fly, and began relieving himself.

Horses snorted in the corral. As he leaned to look around the corner, a pack of horses thundered across the parade grounds, reins slapping their hides, encouraging them onward in a hard run. Although it was dark as sin, Fargo made out the forms of six riders leaning low over their mounts' necks. They were headed south.

Fargo stepped out and watched them disappear, now knowing something was amiss. He glanced at the guardhouse.

A voice shrilled, "Help! The prisoners have escaped."

## 10

Fargo hurried to the guardhouse. Another voice shouted from the corral, "Apache! Apache! Apache are in the camp!" A bugle blared, calling the troopers to arms. Lamps were lit throughout the camp. Barracks emptied quickly. Men dressed as they ran to the corral to saddle their horses.

Fargo found a corporal bracing himself on the woodwork in the guardhouse doorway. Blood trickled down his face from a head wound. Fargo saw that the connecting door stood wide open. In the background the troopers had assembled on the parade grounds. Sergeants shouted their names. Obviously somebody else knew the Apache weren't responsible, Fargo thought. He helped the corporal to a chair and seated him.

Daubing the head wound with his neckerchief, the corporal explained, "The one called Cooney, he did it. It was my fault, though. I should've known better than to go in that cell alone. The major will drum me out of the army, for sure."

"Maybe not," Fargo muttered.

Major Benton strode into the guardhouse, followed by Babcock and a private. Upon seeing blood Benton dispatched the private to fetch Captain White. "Tell him to come here when he's finished with the man at the corral," Benton told the lad. He glanced at Fargo, then to the open connecting door and finally at the corporal and asked, "What happened here?"

Fargo spoke first. "They rode south, Major."

Benton told Babcock, "You heard him, Sergeant. Tell Lieutenant Croft to take a detachment." Babcock hurried away. Benton returned to the corporal. "Son, I'm waiting," he said.

"We had chicken for supper," the corporal began. "Sometimes prisoners save food to eat later on."

Benton rubbed his face, ordered, "Get on with it, Corporal. I haven't the time to hear it verse and rhyme."

"Yes, sir. I heard them banging on the bars and hollering for me to come quick, that a man was dying. I went to see. One of the civilian prisoners, Hank, was on the floor carrying on something awful, choking, gasping and all that, holding his throat. Anyhow, I unlocked the cell and went in to help. Private McRae grabbed me from behind. Cooney busted me good on the head. When I came to, they were gone. All of them."

Major Benton stepped into the doorway, clasped his hands at the small of his back, and lamented, "Mr. Fargo, I knew you were trouble the minute I saw you. Have the governor write all the goddamn letters he wants. I want you out of Camp Stockton immediately. Don't come back." He moved aside to let Captain White enter.

Sergeant Babcock and a private followed White into the room. Benton told Babcock to tell the duty officer to send a replacement for the wounded corporal.

White reported as he cleaned and bandaged the head wound. "They waylayed the sentry at the corral. They're armed to the teeth, Major. While three saddled horses, McRae took the others to his barracks, knocked out the man on duty and absconded with weapons. . . . What are you doing here, Mr. Fargo?"

"He was just leaving," Benton snorted.

Fargo had heard enough. He nodded and left. When he got back to their campsite, he found Apache standing at the edge of the springs. "What was all the commotion about?" she asked. "Horses charging south awakened me. Then another group went the same way. What's up?"

"Hank, Cooney, and four from the army broke out. Benton sent a detachment to catch and bring them back. He also declared us persona non grata in his camp. I'll saddle the horses while you wake the girl and load up the mule."

While they worked, Fargo voiced his opinion on where the escapees were headed, and why. "Hank and Cooney heard us talking about Scoggins and all that money. My guess is they told the others. Surely Private McRae and his buddies know the fastest route to Boquillas."

"Jesus, Fargo, do you realize what you're saying?"

He did indeed. "Think you and me can hog-tie thirteen unwilling desperadoes? I think not."

"I agree." Securing Lulu's trailing rope to her pommel, she went on, "We'll catch as many as we can. Okay by you?"

"We'll see how it works out. Don't count on bringing any back alive, though." He put sleepy Pilar in the saddle, then eased up into it behind her. Bracing her with one arm, she went back to sleep quickly.

Dawn erupted over the prairie, bringing the heat waves and dust devils in its wake. Fargo rode in the tracks left by the escapees and Lieutenant Croft's men. At noon they saw barren mountain peaks on the horizon to their left and right.

"We're now on the Comanche War Trail," she told him. "The peaks are the tops of the Glass Mountains."

At midafternoon they passed through a cut in the ranges. Up close, Fargo saw there was no comparing these mountains to those in the Rockies. These were mere foothills, and barren ones at that, heat sinks absorbing the sun's brutally hot rays. As he scanned those on his left up ahead, he saw a ball of black smoke rise from the top of the highest one. Indians were signaling to others of Fargo and Apache's presence.

Apache had seen the puff of smoke, too. She clarified, "Comanche. Apache around here don't use smoke signals."

Fargo watched a second black cloud float skyward, then there were no more. Undaunted, he rode onward and out of the cut. The Glass Mountains were behind them now. A single mountain—humpbacked, Fargo thought—loomed in the far distance ahead. The many hoofprints he followed were headed straight for it.

He reined to a halt shortly before sunset. They were still short of the humpbacked mountain. "No fire," he told Apache.

"Fargo, they know we're here."

"It will be dark soon. I don't want a fire pinpointing us for them."

He lowered Pilar to the ground, dismounted, and walked over a low rise to scan the distance. While doing so, he saw a group of riders coming toward him. He flattened himself on the ground and shouted to Apache, "Riders coming in. Get the mule and horses down. I'm coming to you." Taking a last look, he started crawling over the rise.

Apache had done what he said. She and Pilar were hunkered down between the horses. "How many?" she asked.

"Too far away to count. But enough to make things hot for us." He withdrew his Sharps from its saddle case and went back and lay atop the rise.

The group came closer. Fargo sighted down the Sharps' barrel, focused on the lead rider, and waited for him to come within range. Applying pressure to the trigger, he saw it was the army detachment, and swung the rifle off his target. He stood and waved to them, shouted to Apache, "Breathe easy. It's the army." He walked back to the horses.

The detachment, Lieutenant Croft and seven troopers, rode up to him and halted. Sitting easy in his saddle, Croft said, "I saw your horse and mule back at camp. You must be Fargo." He glanced at Apache and Pilar. "Where are you folks headed? This particular piece of real estate is crawling with Comanche."

"Boquillas," Fargo answered. "Earlier, we saw their smoke signals."

"Mister, I wouldn't try to make it to Boquillas, if I were you. I'm telling you there are a hell of a lot of savages up ahead. That's why we broke off chasing those six. By now the Comanche have their scalps. I suggest you turn around and go back to Stockton with us. We'll ride all night if we have to."

Fargo looked at Apache and raised his eyebrows, implying it was her decision. She said, "We've come this far."

Croft squalled, "Lady, it's suicide to think you can get past what lies ahead. I've fought 'em, so I know."

"I have, too," she replied. "Many times."

"Well, you can't say I didn't try," Croft answered wryly. "It's ya'll's scalps."

"We'll take our chances," Fargo told him. "We have bigger fish to fry."

Chuckling, Lieutenant Croft touched the brim of his hat, waved, and rode north, shouting, "Follow me, you weary men."

They watched the troopers be swallowed in their own dust. As the hoofbeats faded away, Apache said, "Fargo, one of us may die shortly. Maybe, maybe not."

He loosened the Ovaro's cinch, wondering what suddenly brought on all the gloomy talk. It wasn't like Apache to even consider the dark side of life. "Cheer up, Isabel. Neither of us is going to die. Not on this trip, anyway."

Loosening El Negro's cinch, she expanded on what she was saying. "There's something I have to confess, something I've observed about you." She paused and looked at him from over the Ovaro. "Oh, God, Fargo. I thought I could say it and now I cannot."

He reckoned she wanted to tell him she loved him. So many of his females did.

And the tall Apache woman did, only in an oblique way, one that she herself didn't realize was a testimony of her love for him. Apache paid him a compliment. "No, I have to say it," she spoke more to herself than to him. She cleared her throat and went on. "Fargo, for all you're toughness—and you *are* tough—you're the most gentle man I've ever known, and that includes Will Garrison. Like him, you're also respectful, especially toward females. Not once have you touched me or tried to force yourself on me, not even when I was vulnerable. For those things, I thank you.

"That little girl over there, you took her in without giving it any thought. Held her close, shared your saddle with her, slept with her, and fed her and protected her. Pilar sensed your gentleness, felt your caring.

"What's more important—and it is the trait of yours that I've felt and appreciated most—is your quickness to ask my opinion on matters that affect me. Most men believe women have no brains. You don't. Take the lieutenant, as an example. He said it was suicide for us to continue. And he might very well prove to be right. You turned to me, brought me into the decision-making by asking my opinion with your facial expression. I appreciated that silent display of thoughtfulness. That's what I wanted to say to you. Pilar and I appreciate you, Fargo, because you care."

He wanted to reach over the pinto and pull her to him, embrace and kiss the woman, but mumbled instead, "If you had gone back with them, I'd have finished what we started out to do."

She reached and touched her palm to his cheek. Breaking into a smile, she said, "See? That's what I meant."

He waited for her to explain, but she got a tin of beans instead.

The next day passed without incident until shortly before sundown. They wouldn't have found the trooper were it not for his horse standing nearby. The man lay facedown in greasewood. His clothing was blood-soaked. Two arrows protruded from his back. When the man groaned, Fargo and Apache dismounted and went to him.

"Comanche arrows," Apache muttered.

Fargo turned the trooper on his side and asked, "Can you hear me?"

The soldier's eyes batted open. It was obvious he was near death.

"Tell us what happened," Apache said in a soothing tone of voice.

The man gasped in a weak voice, "Comanche attacked when . . . when we were . . . riding back. On lookout . . . Boquillas."

"Major Benton said he had men watching for the Scoggins gang. Did you see them? Are they in the village?"

"Yes . . . they are there. The Comanche . . ." His eyes closed, his body fell limp.

Fargo knew the soldier was dead. Rising from his squat, he looked toward the flat-topped mountain they had been watching since midafternoon. A smoke signal blossomed from atop it. He said, "We will wait here till dark, then try to thread our way through them. If we move quietly, chances are good they won't hear and find us."

They buried the trooper, set his horse free to roam, then sat and waited for nightfall. Passing the base of the mountain, she told him, "There are small mountains ahead. A place called Persimmon Gap runs between them. Can't miss it, Fargo. Then we're clear all the way to the village."

The large flat-top mountain was behind them now, and they entered the smaller ones. They still carried the sounds of drumbeats. Fargo dismounted and rearranged Lulu's load to ensure silence. All that would be needed to alert the Comanche was for one of the canteens to fall and hit a rock.

About halfway through Persimmon Gap they saw the glow of several Comanche fires. The drumming grew louder. They could hear the Indians chanting in time with the drumbeat. The encampment was close, too damn close for Fargo. He angled right and hugged the far side of the gap's contour.

When they broke out of the gap and Fargo believed the danger of discovery was past, the Comanche pounced. A dozen or more screaming warriors on ponies launched a nocturnal attack.

Fargo yelled, "Make a run for it, Apache." He turned the Ovaro, drew his Colt, and charged into the Comanche. He shot two off their mounts, wheeled, and got a third.

Apache's Colt barked twice. She had ignored him

and joined in the melee. The Comanche warriors were all around them, swinging tomahawks and pogamoggans, slashing at them with knives. Fargo shot a club-wielding warrior off his pony. Hugging Pilar close, he missed on his next shot, but hit flesh on his last. Holstering the Colt, he drew his Sharps and began knocking Indians to the ground with its barrel. Apache's Colt continued to fire. He fired blindly into the Comanche swarming all around him. A cloud of dust formed by all the furious activity made it even harder for him to see. The bullwhip started cracking. He knew Apache's gun was empty and she was now beating them off. He angled toward the sound of the bullwhip and rode in to help her.

She was on the ground between El Negro and Lulu, fighting off two pony-mounted warriors who were twisting and turning to avoid the whip. Fargo returned the empty Sharps to its saddle case and withdrew his Arkansas toothpick. Charging the two warriors, he stabbed one in the chest, wheeled around, and slashed the other's arm. The man screamed, then fled.

Fargo quickly reloaded the Colt and waited for the confused warriors to find them and come. But they had broken off their attack. He heard their war whoops as they rode for the hills.

He handed Pilar to Apache, dismounted, and said, "Are you all right? Hurt?"

Coiling the bullwhip, she answered, "I'm fine. That was close. They damn near scared the daylights out of poor Lulu. She was bucking and kicking and hee-hawing her lungs out. Kicked a pony so hard that it jarred the warrior off."

Fargo looked at the lop-eared mule. She still seemed a tad nervous from the ordeal. He got one of the canteens and drank his fill. "I don't want to have that to do again."

"What?"

Jamming a cork stopper back in place, he told her, "Fight while holding the girl. There were times I needed both hands free. She's lucky she didn't get killed."

"Did you notice some of them carried new carbines?"

"Yes. They wouldn't use them fighting in close range. The knives, hatchets, and war clubs were better." He climbed back into the saddle and took Pilar from her.

Riding away at a gallop, Apache said, "I'll see if I can find an old friend to watch after the girl while we're busy in Boquillas."

At midnight Fargo reined to halt at the east end of what Apache said was Chisos Basin. After eating beans and the leftover chicken, they opened their bedrolls and got some sleep. Apache had told him they were only a few miles from the border.

Fargo's inner clock awakened him at four in the morning. He wanted to be on the north bank of the river at dawn.

At first light, Fargo started watching the ground for hoofprints. Though they hadn't seen or heard any Comanche since leaving Persimmon Gap, that didn't mean they weren't around. He saw no hoofprints.

Apache asked, "Do you want to see the village, look it over, before riding in? I think you should."

When he agreed, she angled right. Minutes later they rode up on the northern rim of a narrow canyon carved by the Rio Grande. The village stood a short distance on the other side. They dismounted and started studying the village.

Pointing, Apache said, "The large building is the *federales'* headquarters, when they are here. Only they aren't around. If they were, their flag would be flying."

Fargo focused on the building. It was box-shaped and had two levels. Inside the box would be a courtyard. A wide balcony supported by columns ran completely around the upper level. Several horses stood at hitching rails in front of the adobe structure. Facing the headquarters was a mission having a bell tower. The mission was much smaller than the headquarters. Separating the two was a rather large open area. A labyrinth of narrow streets lined with flat-topped roofs of adobe hovels was behind the mission, the corral used by the *federales* behind the headquarters building. Individual adobe homes dotted the outskirts of Boquillas. They were outside a tumbledown wall that encompassed three sides of the village. Smoke from cooking fires hung over the village.

Roosters on the wall exchanged crows. The bell began tolling, calling the people to morning Mass. As Fargo watched, the first villagers emerged from the maze and went into the mission.

Apache nudged him and nodded for him to look down and to his right.

Six riders were fording the river below. One wore chaps.

# 11

Fargo watched the six escapees cross the Rio Grande and halt short of the village. After obviously discussing things, they turned right, away from the headquarters, and started to move around the village. Fargo said, "They saw the gang's horses and have decided to sneak up unseen from the west. We'd best hurry before they kill off some of the Scoggins boys." He reined right and started to go back down the northern slope of the canyon wall.

Apache stopped him, saying, "No, Fargo. I know a shorter, faster way." She reined left, he followed.

After going a short distance, she led him into a maze of crevices barely wider than their horses—so tight, in fact, that both she and Fargo had to keep their feet on the saddles in order for their mounts to negotiate the exceedingly narrow twists and turns in the steep, downward conduit. He suspected the gang had also found the shortcut and used it to bypass the troopers keeping watch over the village.

Nearing the river, she told him, "Get ready to swim. You'll see a wide crack in the canyon wall on the other side. Head for it. It leads to the top of the wall."

When Fargo negotiated the last turn, he saw Apache had left her saddle but held on the pommel while the horse and mule effected the crossing. He told Pilar to wrap her arms around his neck and hang on. He slid off the saddle, bringing her with him. The Ovaro stepped off the sharp incline and entered the water. Fargo grabbed and hung on to the saddle horn. By the time the Ovaro had made it halfway across, Apache was astride El Negro, taking the mule into the crack.

From the top of the south rim the village looked bigger. They were to the northeast of the headquarters building, fully exposed in open terrain.

Apache said what Fargo thought, "We can't leave Pilar here in the opening. They might get away from us, come straight to the shortcut, and their horses would trample her. Wait here. I'll take her to Mass and leave her with somebody."

Fargo watched her pull a black dress from a bundle carried by Lulu. Slipping it over her other clothes, she asked, "What's the plan, Fargo?"

He glanced from the building to the mission to the village proper, then back to the building. Finally, he said, "We know the gang is in the building and the escapees are probably in position to come over the west wall. While you are going to the mission, I'll leave the horses and mule here and go behind the building. By that time it's reasonable to believe the escapees will have worked their way to behind the mission. So, just before going behind the headquarters, I'll wait for you to appear in the mission doorway, then signal for you to fire a shot. That shot should intimidate the escapees and give them ample cause to change their plans. You can count on Scoggins' men to pour outside to see what in the hell's going on. When they do, I'll fire a shot from the rear of the building. That will certainly confuse everybody. They will run back inside to meet the new threat. When they do, you run to the building, come inside, and get the drop on as many as you can. I'll enter from the rear and do the same. How does the plan sound to you?"

"Like a pile of horse apples. But it's better than none."

"Yeah, well, if it doesn't work out, we'll do the best we can, play it by ear. Good hunting."

She nodded, picked up Pilar and the bag of pigging ropes, and started walking.

Fargo moved the horses and Lulu away from the opening, withdrew the Sharps, and double-checked that it and his Colt were fully loaded, then headed for the back of the building. As he walked, he scanned the windows and doors for movement inside and glanced occasionally at the corners of the mission to maybe spot the escapees. He made it to the corner of the building at the same time Apache entered the mission.

The sun made its debut on the new day, bringing a wind with it, one that churned dust devils between the mission and the building behind which Fargo stood, waiting impatiently for Apache to appear in the mission's entrance.

Cooney stepped from behind the mission, took a fast look at the headquarters, then withdrew.

A few minutes later Cooney and two of the wayward troopers emerged from behind the mission and hugged its wall while moving forward. Fargo was sure the others were doing likewise on the other side. Cooney peered around the front corner of the mission at the same time Hank peered around the other. They saw Apache step partway through the doorway. She'd shucked her dress and drawn her gun. Her right hand held the bullwhip. The bag lay at her feet.

Hank raised his weapon and aimed at her. Fargo took a bead on him with the Sharps and squeezed the trigger. The bullet hit Hank in the chest, catapulted him backward. Before Fargo could swing and fire at Cooney, the outlaw started running, zigzagging across the square. He shot while running. Twice, his bullets knocked chinks out to the upright column just inches above Fargo's head. Cooney swerved to his right and disappeared in front of the building.

Fargo dropped one of the four army men and was swinging onto another when a whirlwind blasted into him. Swirling dust temporarily blinded him.

He heard boots running on the balcony above him. A male voice shouted, "What in hell's going on, Buddy?"

Buddy yelled back, "Christ, I don't know. Troopers?"

Gunfire erupted at the front of the building. Fargo glanced that way, then beyond, to Apache still standing in the mission's doorway. She would be trapped until all activity in front of headquarters ceased.

He pulled back behind the column and reloaded the

Sharps. When he peered around it again, he saw one of the army boys had made it safely to under the balcony. He stood next to the wall with his back to Fargo. His right hand gripped a six-gun. The fellow peeked around the corner, obviously saw one of the gang members, and opened fire.

Fargo knew his basic plan, which Apache had so candidly called horse apples, was shot to hell. The element of surprise had been lost. He decided to stay out of it and let the two groups fight it out, and thus thin their numbers. He would stay behind the column and not shoot unless discovered. Fargo had a clear view of the rear and right side of the building, Apache its front and left side. He kept his powder dry and waited for her to make the next move.

The trooper Fargo was watching pulled back and ran to the first window he came to. After trying to raise it, he broke the glass, raised the window, and climbed inside. Seconds later Fargo heard gunfire within the structure. After a brief exchange, it suddenly got quiet inside.

Fargo heard Leonard holler, "You okay, Addie?"

Bad Addie answered, "Yeah! Caught him crossing the courtyard. How're you guys doing?"

"They got Alex," Leonard answered. "Watch yourself, Addie. There's several more of them inside."

As Leonard spoke, another exchange of gunfire erupted, this time on the second level. Fargo heard a voice cry, "Ow! I'm hit. I'm hit. Help me, somebody."

He heard boots run on the inner balcony. Gang members were closing in on the gunmen who shot one of their own.

Leonard yelled, "Buddy! Where are you, Buddy? Where is the bastard?"

Buddy didn't answer. Three shots did. "Get him, boys," Leonard growled. Several six-guns opened fire simultaneously. Leonard's voice roared over the gunfire, "Stop shooting. We got him."

Bad Addie shouted, "They're getting away. Two of them. On the square."

Fargo looked that way, saw Cooney and the one

surviving trooper running across the square. Bad Addie's bullets kicked up tiny dust devils at their feet as they skirted the mission on the right side of it. He saw Apache look up at the second level, snatch the bag off the floor, then run from the doorway and chase after Cooney and his companion. As he watched, two of the gang sprinted across the square. Apache was in jeopardy.

Fargo brought the Sharps' stock to his shoulder and aimed at the lead runner. The impact of the Sharps slug knocked the man facedown on the ground. The other runner stumbled over the dead man and fell. When he rose on his knees and looked behind, Fargo squeezed off another round. The bullet tore a hunk from the man's skull. Blood and brains flew in all directions.

Bad Addie shouted, "There's something funny going on, fellows."

It appeared to Fargo that any chance of capturing them was now out of the question. They would discover him soon enough. He opted to take them head-on and dashed to the open window and crawled over the sill. The room had a musty smell, as though it had been locked up too long. Scant light spilled through the window and the doorway to the courtyard. As he crossed the room, a wooden chest setting in the middle of a long table jammed against the wall next to the door caught his eye. He stepped to the table and opened the lid to the chest. It was three-quarters filled with jewelry of every description, mostly necklaces with crucifixes. He dug a hand in them, lifted, and let the jewelry trickle between his fingers. Cash, lots of it, covered the chest's bottom.

Fargo moved next to the doorway and peered out into the courtyard. The trooper's twisted body lay over the near rim of a circular pool. Movement on the inner balcony drew Fargo's attention. Glancing up, he drew his Colt and thumbed back the hammer.

Leonard Ray Scoggins darted from one door and entered another. Fargo shot at him but missed, the round knocking wood out of the framework of the second door. He heard boots scrape on the balcony above his head. Leonard poked his gun around one side of the doorway and fired twice at Fargo. Fargo pulled back in the nick of time. Both bullets ricocheted off the tile floor and thudded into the wall below the window.

Leonard shouted, "We have him now. Clarence, you go one way, Addie, the other."

Fargo heard them on the balcony, one moving left, the other to the right. He looked at the window, then headed to it. Outside, he rushed to the front door. After peering inside and seeing nobody, he stepped into the foyer and crossed to an archway leading into the courtyard. Clarence was creeping next to the wall below the courtyard balcony, his eyes and sawed-off shotgun aimed on the doorway Fargo had just left. Bad Addie edged along the wall facing Clarence. Fargo selected Dowd. He wanted the son of a bitch in the worst way, anyhow. But he wouldn't dry-gulch the man. Fargo stepped into the archway and said, "Looking for me?"

Their surprise was complete. Both outlaws spun to face him. Dowd fired first and missed. A tight pattern of buckshot from both barrels tore off a section of the archway. Bad Addie's bullet breezed past Fargo's left ear. He shot Clarence Dowd in the heart. Bad Addie swung into the open doorway as he fired at her. The bullet dug into the framework. "You're next, Leonard Ray," Fargo yelled.

Leonard emptied his cylinder at the sound of Fargo's voice. The bullets kissed off the wall below the balcony and whined away harmlessly. Fargo ran to the stairway Bad Addie had used, taking them three steps at a time, and raced to catch Leonard before he got reloaded. Bad Addie's bullets hit the wall behind and in front of him. He cooked off a round to intimidate her . . . and heard Apache's bullwhip crack. Bad Addie screamed.

Now knowing that Apache was in the room with her, protecting his backside, Fargo focused all his attention on Leonard. Halting beside the doorway, Fargo called to him, "You can have it one of two ways, Scoggins. Easy and live, or hard and die."

"Fuck you," Leonard Ray snarled, and sent two shots screaming through the doorway.

Fargo slid down the wall, rolled onto his stomach, and fired twice. Both bullets hammered into Leonard's chest. He was dead before he hit the floor. Fargo stood and shouted, "You all right, Apache?"

"Yes," she answered. "I've got her hog-tied."

He went down to see. Bad Addie lay unconscious on the floor. He asked, "Cooney and the trooper?"

"I have Cooney tied up in the mission. The army boy wanted to shoot it out, made me kill him. Any wounded?"

"No," he muttered as a war-painted face behind a carbine appeared in the window.

Two others, flanked by at least a dozen more, stepped through the doorway. Fargo and Apache were disarmed and shoved into the courtyard. A warrior draped Bad Addie over his shoulder and headed for the archway. Warriors herded Fargo and Apache out front. The square was filled with Comanche. Terrified females shrieked within the village proper. The hot wind carried much dust. Two warriors dragged Cooney from the mission and left him at Fargo's feet. The one carrying Bad Addie dumped her on the ground next to Cooney. The crowd of Indians parted. A powerfully built Comanche wearing a war bonnet rode through the gap and halted a few feet away from the captives.

"I am Nocona, Chief of the Comanche," he said in good English. He slid off his pony and stepped to Apache. Grabbing a fistful of her hair, Nocona pulled her to her knees and said, "I claim this one as my slave."

"No, you won't," Fargo replied. "She's my captive. All of them are my captives. The man also."

Nocona stepped in front of Fargo and put the end of his carbine's barrel under Fargo's chin and said, "White man, you are my prisoner. Be silent. Speak only when I tell you to." He looked at Bad Addie and rolled her faceup with his foot. He noticed that her wrists were bound and that Cooney was tied hand and foot. Nocona glanced at Fargo and grunted, "Why are these two tied and not the Apache woman?"

"I was about to tie her up when your warriors arrived," Fargo answered.

Chief Nocona mounted up. He gave an order in Comanche to the warriors. They immediately formed into a large circle on the square. A pony-mounted warrior gestured for Fargo to go inside the circle. Nocona grunted a command. A tall, muscular warrior dismounted and moved into the circle. Dust swirled around the two men. All was quiet.

Finally, Nocona spoke. "White man, if what you say about them being your prisoners is true, then you will live. If not, then you will die. I do not know what is true or lie. Only the spirits know." Nocona half-moved a hand.

A warrior carrying a coil of braided horsehair entered the circle. Fargo knew at once what was about to happen. He took off his hat, neckerchief, and shirt and tossed them onto the ground, out of the way. Then he reached down and withdrew the Arkansas toothpick from its calf sheath and stood waiting. The warrior tied one end of the braid to Fargo's left wrist and the other to the muscular warrior's. A tomahawk was given to Fargo's combatant. The braid separated the two by about six feet.

A large dust devil broke around the warrior facing Fargo and blasted into him and his adversary. The fight began in the swirl. Fargo yanked the braid. The other man had anticipated the jerk and had taken a pace forward. The braid fell slack momentarily, then tightened as they began circling, sizing each other up, testing for an opening.

The warrior lunged and slashed the tomahawk at Fargo's head.

He ducked under it and stabbed for the warrior's belly. The warrior danced away. The braid grew taut, but only briefly.

The warrior feigned left, pulling on the braid at the same time.

Fargo lost his balance, stumbled, and fell.

The warrior pounced.

Fargo glimpsed the onrushing steel blade of the tomahawk. He rolled onto his right side and grabbed the tomahawk's handle. Wrenching it out of the man's hand, Fargo pulled him to the ground.

For a split second their breaths mixed. Then Fargo hit him in the face with the end of the stiletto's handle. The warrior grunted, fell away, and started scrambling to his feet. Fargo wrapped the braid around the warrior's neck and pulled him back to the ground. Planting a knee in the red man's stomach, Fargo put the sharp tip of the stiletto under the man's chin.

One shove on the stiletto and the warrior would die. Fargo glanced at Nocona. The chief's expression never changed. Apparently he didn't care if his warrior lived or died. Fargo nicked the warrior's flesh, just enough to produce a bead of blood, then took the blade away and stood. He pulled the warrior to his feet and embraced him.

Both turned to face Chief Nocona and waited for his decision.

Nocona grunted, "Why didn't you kill him, white man?"

Fargo replied, "There's been enough killing this day."

Nocona stared at him. Finally, he said, "The spirits say the captives belong to you, white man. Take them and leave."

The circle of riders parted. Fargo went to Apache and said, "Go get Pilar. Nocona is letting us go." He told Cooney and Bad Addie to stay on the ground, "If you want to live." Then he whistled to the Ovaro.

The Comanche didn't believe their eyes when the powerful black-and-white pinto stallion, followed by El Negro and Lulu, trotted up to Fargo. He shot a wink to the warrior he'd fought, then stepped to and unhitched a pair of the gang's horses.

Apache returned with Pilar and asked, "What about our guns and my bullwhip?"

First, Fargo motioned for Cooney and Bad Addie to

get in their saddles, then he approached Chief Nocona and made the request, explaining, "Chief, we have a long and dangerous ride ahead of us."

Chief Nocona broke a grin when he agreed. "White man, you walk in danger. It's all around you." He grunted an order to a warrior.

The man disappeared inside the *federales'* headquarters for a short time. He came back with the weapons and her bullwhip. Fargo started to mount up. It suddenly occurred to him they were leaving the chest behind. Telling Apache to get in her saddle with Pilar, he dashed to the room and came back with the chest. Nocona watched him tie it to Lulu. Fargo held his breath while mounting up. But the chief never inquired about what the chest contained.

Fargo put the Ovaro's rump to the Comanche, Boquillas del Carmen, the heat-seared Big Bend country, and slowly rode away.

# 12

Inasmuch as they no longer had a reason to return to Camp Stockton, Fargo and Apache took their prisoners and Pilar in a straight line from Boquillas to Austin. At high noon on the second day the Rio Grande once again came into view. They found a shallow place to ford and halted. Fargo took Cooney upstream to bathe and wash their clothes, while Apache went downstream with Pilar and Bad Addie to do the same. When they finished, they met on the Texas side of the great river and made camp.

"Any trouble with her?" Fargo asked, nodding toward Bad Addie.

"None at all," Apache replied.

"They're too quiet, have been since we left Boquillas," he said.

"Think they're up to something?"

"Could be. It's not like those two to go quietly. Starting here and now, we better keep them separated. And I'm more concerned about Bad Addie than him."

Fargo tied Cooney to a scrub oak. Cooney didn't resist. Getting his Sharps, Fargo told Apache, "Going upstream to get us a deer. I saw their tracks earlier.

"I'll make a fire and have everything ready when you get back," she said. She watched him walk the bank.

He found the deer tracks easily enough: four doe and a buck. Fargo started tracking his quarry, pausing occasionally to check the wind direction. After going almost a mile, he spotted one of the doe less than fifty yards away, grazing among post oak. He lowered to the ground and got into firing position. When he swung the barrel around ever so slowly, the doe became alert and looked right at him. Then he saw the buck facing him from a cluster of rocks to the left of the post oak. He inched the barrel around, aimed at the buck, and shot him through the heart.

He brought it back field-stripped. Apache had the fire going. She took over when he lowered the deer from his shoulders. "Eight points," she said, "nice and plump."

Fargo sat and watched her skin the buck, then carve venison steaks. He noticed she'd tied Bad Addie to Lulu and the mule to a tree far enough away from Cooney that neither could speak without her or Fargo hearing. Pilar squatted on the beach, chunking rocks into the water. Apache had fashioned skewers out of slender mesquite limbs. Soon the unmistakable aroma of roasting venison wafted over the Rio Grande. Fargo fed and watered their captives first.

Midway through the meal, Bad Addie whined, "I need a man. I prefer you, big man, but Cooney will do."

Apache stabbed her skewer in the ground and tilted the piece of venison over the fire. Bad Addie watched her pull off her neckerchief and walked toward her.

"You ain't gonna gag me, you Indian whore," Bad Addie hissed.

"You shouldn't have called her that," Fargo muttered, and he took another bite of venison.

He watched Apache untie Bad Addie. "Go ahead, Adeline, rub life into your wrists, then I'm going to give you the beating of your life. It's long overdue, anyhow."

Bad Addie laughed and dropped into a crouch, saying, "Ain't no whore alive that can whup my ass. You stay out of it, big man. After I choke the bitch to death, you and me will screw proper like."

"Hunh," Fargo snorted, "if you beat Apache, I'll give back your gear and set you free. But I won't lie with you."

Bad Addie lunged with arms outspread. Apache

sidestepped. Bad Addie's left finger gouged Apache's right trouser leg. Apache's fist shot out and hit the other woman's shoulder a glancing blow. Bad Addie spun to face her and began weaving, taunting the taller woman, encouraging her to come to her, snarling, "Bitch. Rotten Apache whore."

Apache swung a left hook. Bad Addie ducked it and threw a left jab that caught Apache's jaw. She staggered backward, shaking her head. Bad Addie followed with a blow to the abdomen that doubled Apache over. Bent over, Apache covered her face and weaved left to right, taking the sting out of Bad Addie's flying fists.

An uppercut by Bad Addie stunned Apache. Her knees buckled, she reeled into Lulu's side and sunk to her knees. Bad Addie grabbed a fistful of her long hair and positioned Apache's face for the knockout. Bad Addie cocked her right fist and snarled, "Bye-bye, bitch."

Fargo saw Apache's hands shoot up and throw dirt in her adversary's face. Bad Addie let go of her hair and reeled, temporarily blinded and sputtering. Apache staggered to her feet, slammed a right into the blinded woman's gut. A lungful of air gushed from Bad Addie's mouth. She fell forward, taking Apache to the ground with her. Coming to her knees, Apache pulled her up and drove a right fist square to Bad Addie's mouth and nose. Blood spurted from Bad Addie's upper lip and gushed from her nose. Apache hit her again, this time with a left to the right eye.

Bad Addie's senses were fading; still she swung. One of her blindly thrown punches connected on Apache's right cheek, another on her lower lip. Both places split open. Blood streaked down the cheek, spurted from the lip. Both females panted, were near exhaustion. Apache made it to her feet. Bad Addie clutched her legs. Breathing hard, Apache pulled the woman's head back and hit her in the mouth again. Bad Addie collapsed, out cold.

Fargo pitched Apache his neckerchief, which he had

dampened with the river's water. "One of the better brawls I've seen in a month of Sundays."

She sat on the saddle to wipe blood off her face. "Now I know why they call her Bad Addie. Would you have really let her go?"

"No. I'd have shot her in the leg. Cooney, too. Hear that, Cooney boy?"

"Yeah, I heard," he drawled. "You wanna take me on in a fair fight?"

Fargo looked at Apache and asked, "Does he mean me or you?"

She pulled Bad Addie's limp body to the saddle and wiped her face. As she did, Fargo noticed Apache's tongue feel over the busted lower lip. He said, "Good thing you're not the kissing type. That lip will be tender for quite a spell."

Her eyes kicked up to his, the only indication that she heard him. She went back to cleaning Bad Addie's face.

Fargo took the neckerchief from her and went to the river to wet it anew. When he came back, he said, "Here, let me have a look at your scrapes and bruises." She tilted her head and watched his eyes while he cleaned. He allowed, "You're puffy around the left eye. The gash on your cheek might leave a thin scar. Other than that you're okay."

She didn't comment, just gagged Bad Addie, then tied her to the mule, then tried to eat her venison steak. Fargo wanted to reach over and hug her, but pulled Pilar to him instead.

Bad Addie groaned and stirred into consciousness. Sitting, she stared at Apache.

Apache warned, "I gagged you for your own good. Call me either of those names again and I'll kill you."

Night fell without further incident. Pilar slept with her Aunt Isabel while Fargo watched over their captives and nibbled venison steak. After a while he moved out of range of the dim firelight and went to sleep sitting with his back to an oak.

Dawn found them riding single-file, with Fargo in

the lead. Shortly after sunrise they entered the Texas hill country.

Apache teased, "Hey, Fargo, shall we make a detour, go back to Fredericksburg to see if that German farmer caught up with his daughters?"

He laughed, but didn't dare comment.

In midafternoon, three days later, they rode into Austin. A crowd of gawkers surrounded and followed them to the sheriff's office. "Who you bring back this time, Apache?" a man shouted. "That one looks like a female," another yelled. "What did they do?" another asked. And so it went all the way to the sheriff's office.

The sheriff, an older man but brawny, and his lean deputy stepped out front as they dismounted. "Howdy, Apache," the sheriff said in a whiskey voice. "Heard you went hunting in west Texas. What'cha got for me?"

Fargo motioned Cooney and Bad Addie to get out of their saddles.

Apache explained, "Two bad ones, Sheriff Walker. Cooney Roberts and Adeline Scoggins. Some call her Bad Addie. They are to be held for trial. Cooney on charges of armed robbery, and Bad Addie on charges of extortion and murder, among others."

"Who'd he rob?" the deputy wanted to know. "And who did she kill?"

Fargo shoved Cooney forward and said, "A Butterfield stage." Yanking Bad Addie's leash, he continued. "Her list of crimes is long."

David Winston bulled his way through the crowd and came to Fargo. Beaming, David pumped Fargo's hand, saying to Sheriff Walker, "Lock them up, Walker." He hugged Apache. On pulling back, he noticed her lip wound and asked, "How did you come by that?" He glanced at Fargo, as though he were responsible.

Apache chuckled. "No, Senator, Fargo didn't do it. Adeline Scoggins did. She had a speech problem."

"Well, well," Senator Winston began cheerily, "come in the office and tell me about your trip. Damn, wish

Will was here to hear it." He gestured for them to precede him into the office.

Both Fargo and Apache turned at the same time. He deferred to her, bowing slightly and saying, "By all means fetch her, Aunt Isabel."

"What's this?" David cleared his throat. "Aunt Isabel?"

Nodding toward Pilar astride the powerful black-and-white, Fargo grinned and said, "I'm Uncle Fargo."

They watched Apache lift her from the saddle. Coming to them, she explained, "She was orphaned in a massacre carried out by the Comanche at Río Pecos. The sole survivor. We tried to find her a new home but alas, to no avail." She glanced at Fargo. "We haven't talked about who will take her."

While the deputy separated Cooney and Adeline in adjoining cells, Fargo and the others sat to talk.

Senator Winston began the discussion. "Tell it from the beginning. Don't leave anything out."

Apache's nod suggested that Fargo start. He said, "We started at Rancho de Sueño, Don Diego Rodriguez's spread. The Scoggins gang had massacred everyone." He went on to tell why he knew the Scoggins gang was responsible, then told what they found at Río Pecos and heard from Manuel before he died. "That's where we found the girl, Pilar." He looked at Apache and asked her to tell what happened next.

Apache told about the Butterfield stage in Crescent Gap. Withdrawing the signed deposition from her pocket, she said, "This is signed by the men Cooney and Hank robbed." She handed it to the sheriff and continued her story through the part about being bit by the rattlesnake. "Fargo can tell you what happened after that."

All eyes went to Fargo, who said, "We went to Camp Stockton." He gave an overview of the events at the camp, including the nighttime escape from the guardhouse. "We headed south immediately, for Boquillas, a village just across the border in Big Bend country, where we suspected the gang was holed up." He went on to tell about the nocturnal attack by

Comanche warriors and what occurred after that. "At dawn we were atop the north rim of a canyon overlooking the village when Apache spotted the escapees fording the river below. She can tell you the rest."

Apache gave them a glowing, most graphic and vivid account about hers and Fargo's movements preceding and during the shoot-out at Boquillas del Carmen. They sat mesmerized throughout the story. "So, we were lucky to have taken Cooney and Bad Addie alive," she concluded.

Fargo added, "Bad Addie can verify what Apache has told you."

"I ain't saying nothin'," Bad Addie shouted from where she stood at the bars.

Walker suggested they step outside. When all were gathered on the porch, Sheriff Walker closed the door and said, "We have a problem regarding that woman. What happened in Mexico is up to the *federales* to resolve. We can't meddle in their business. Right, Senator?"

It was apparent by Winston's body language that he didn't like doing it, but he agreed.

Walker continued. "We can't hold Adeline Scoggins indefinitely. A good lawyer could get her out. Here's why. You have no proof of her part in the crimes at Rancho de Sueño or Río Pecos, only hearsay, your word against hers. That isn't good enough. What it will take to bring her to trial are charges by somebody else, somebody who was victimized by her, an eyewitness to her atrocities. Fargo, I fear you will have to go back to west Texas and find that somebody."

Visions of heat waves rippled in Fargo's skull, dust devils scampered in his mind. He groaned.

Walker said, "All is not lost, though. After all, you and Apache did rid the planet of all of them except Bad Addie. For that we can be grateful. We have no problem with Cooney Roberts. I can assure you he will hang for what he has done. In the meantime, I will hold Adeline as long as I can, buy Fargo as much time as possible while he finishes his work."

Winston cleared his throat. Fargo took it as a signal

of something profound about to be announced. Winston said, "This matter is most urgent, Fargo. When is the earliest you can leave?"

Apache spoke up in his defense. "David, do you realize what you're asking? We're tired. No! More than tired. Exhausted."

Fargo waved her off saying, "I'll leave at dawn tomorrow."

The senator reached inside a vest pocket and withdrew several bills. Handing them to Fargo, he said, "This is the balance due you." Glancing at Apache, he said, "I'll settle up with you later."

She responded, "Keep your money, Senator. I was doing this as a favor. Remember? Without Fargo, I'd be a dead woman. It couldn't have been done without him. Not by me, not by anyone else."

Winston cleared his throat again. After glancing at Apache he shifted to Fargo and offered, "You're welcome to stay with Polly and me until you leave—"

"No," Apache interrupted. "He's staying at my place." She drilled a penetrating stare of defiance into Winston's eyes.

He quickly capitulated.

Fargo grinned and said, "Sheriff, where do we put all the cash and valuables Scoggins stole? It's on the mule, bagged and ready." He led Walker to Lulu and pointed out the bags to him.

While Walker and his deputy carried the bags inside, the senator stepped off the porch and went to Fargo. Shaking the Trailsman's hand, he said, "Good hunting, Fargo. Have a safe and speedy return. If the amount of money isn't enough—"

Fargo hurried to cut him off. "No, Senator, the payment is fine with me. Glad to be of help."

Senator David Winston nodded, turned, and walked away, heading for the capitol building.

Apache sat Pilar in her saddle and eased up behind her. Fargo mounted up and followed her to the ranch. They arrived at sunset. The entire household staff of Mexicans stood out front to greet them. Beaming a wide smile, a young maid eagerly took Pilar when Apache held her down to the woman's loving hands.

Inside, Fargo saw the sprawling ranch house's motif was in keeping with Isabel's heritage, a mixture of Spanish and Apache cultures. He was comfortable at once.

She and a butler walked him to his bedroom door. Before leaving, Apache said, "Roberto will tend to your needs. Roberto, show him where to bathe, then bring him to the dinner table." Turning to Fargo, she said, "After the bedroll, I know you will be pleased in these quarters. Now, I'll share my tub with the little one, and we will have a badly needed hot bath. See you at dinner."

He watched her walk away, then stepped into the spacious bedroom dominated by a raised, massive four-poster bed with a canopy. A low whistle of appreciation escaped his lips as he tested the bed.

The butler, a rotund, jolly, older fellow, said, "If you will excuse me, *señor*, I'll prepare your bath."

"By all means, you're excused."

Fargo moved to and looked out a window and watched the peach-colored sky change to black while he waited for the butler to return to fetch him.

The bedroom door opened quietly and the butler said, "Follow me, *señor*." He led Fargo across the corridor, into a quite large bathroom. Fargo stood looking down into a monstrous tiled vat of steaming water. He stripped and stepped down into it. For the next half-hour he basked with his eyes closed, then he put a soaped washcloth to work and scrubbed the last vestige of smelly creosote from his body.

The manservant held a towel open for him. As Fargo dried off, the fellow gestured toward a fresh set of cleaned and ironed clothing and commented, "Your dinner attire, *señor*. I will have your clothes washed and ironed and put in your bedroom."

He helped Fargo dress in a loose-fitting, white cotton garb. A wide, bright-red sash went around the waist. After combing his hair, Fargo spread his hands and looked at the butler for his approval. The man smiled and nodded, then escorted Fargo to the dining room. He found Apache and Pilar already seated on one side of the long candlelit table. Both females wore white dresses. Their hair was pulled back and held in place by flaming-red Spanish combs. Both of them greeted him with smiles as he sat facing them.

Maids served the individual courses of the sumptuous meal, retiring from the room between each. They ate in leisure, after which the young maid, whom Fargo assumed Apache had assigned to Pilar, took the youngster to her bedroom.

Fargo and Apache lingered at the table awhile longer. Neither spoke as they watched each other nibble sections of oranges and sip their wine. Juice from the sweet oranges covered their lips and trickled down her chin and Fargo's black beard. Slowly their fingers met on the table. No words were needed to convey what each was thinking; their eyes said it all, promised much. Their fingers entwined and squeezed tenderly, lovingly. Her breathing quickened noticeably.

They rose simultaneously from their chairs and held hands while she led him to her bedchamber. There they embraced and kissed for what seemed to him a long time. Pulling back, she slipped the thin straps of her long dress from her shoulders and let the dress fall to the floor, never once moving her eyes off his or altering her serious expression.

He removed the sash, pulled his shirt over his head, and dropped it and his pants to the floor. Removing his boots and socks, he watched her sit on the edge of the bed and swing her long slender legs onto it, then recline and draw one knee up. Her heaving bosom foretold the fiery passion that burned within, begging for release, craving for long-awaited satisfaction.

He lowered his gaze to her flat belly, then farther to her jet-black pubic hair. She slowly parted her legs and beckoned him to enter the bed, and her.

Fargo got in bed, knelt, and spread her legs wider, then bent and kissed each tiny nipple as his throbbing member parted her fever-swollen lower lips. She pulled him to lie on her, reached down, and fed his mushroom-shaped crown into her moist sheath. He kissed her openmouthed as she raised her hips to force penetration.

He entered slowly, knowing that for all practical purposes it was her first time, and as such, her love tunnel would be tight and tender. He felt her knees touch his waist, then her ankles lock on the small of his back. Isabel Sayas was as ready as she ever would be. He thrust his full length inside the hot, moist casing. She grunted once and met his deep plunge by fusing her steaming opening to his base.

His hands went to her buttocks and pulled her tightly to him. Securely mated, he began gyrating. She unlocked her ankles and dug her heels into his hard buttocks, encouraged him to go faster.

He felt her hot breaths on his neck and throat as her insteps found his shoulders. In the new position, her hot crack raised and opened even more for him. Their moist flesh made soft slapping sounds as she bucked concurrent with his hard thrusts.

They were well-lubricated now, and he glided in and out easily. Her feet came back to his buttocks, and she began rotating her hips in the opposite direction of his movements. As her slickened membrane contracted around his manhood, she moaned. He flooded her. She clutched and held him tightly throughout the eruption.

When it was over, her arms and legs lowered onto the bed. He remained atop her until he limbered. Rolling to lie beside her, he put her head on his chest. She kissed his nipples, throat, and eyes, then whispered, "We both needed that, I more than you."

He whispered back, "No, Isabel, we deserved each other. There is a difference. One is created out of necessity, the other out of desire. Any woman can satisfy my sexual needs. Make no mistake about it. Only you could satisfy my immediate sexual desires, and I yours."

She rolled atop him and kissed him hotly. After the kiss, she said, "You don't have to leave in the morning. You can stay and satisfy our desires as long as you wish."

So swiftly we move from desire to need to outright lust, he thought, but said, "I've a job to do and—"

Her fingers touched his lips and cut him off. She explained, "No, Fargo. Hear me out. While Pilar and I bathed, it occurred to me that she might have been an eyewitness to a crime committed by Adeline in Río Pecos."

"So you asked her?" Fargo muttered.

"Yes. She saw Adeline Scoggins kill three people. Two women and a man. I'll take her to Sheriff Walker tomorrow. He can get Irene López to interpret what she has to tell. The sheriff can ask the questions. No jury would dare challenge a four-year-old eyewitness's words."

He gave the matter hardly any thought at all before agreeing. He said, "In that case, I don't have to be in Fort Laramie before next month. Is that long enough to take care of your itch?"

She shot him a wink.

**LOOKING FORWARD!**
The following is the opening
section from the next novel in the exciting
*Trailsman* series from Signet:

**THE TRAILSMAN #105
COUNTERFEIT CARGO**

*1860, where the Montana and Idaho territories
shoulder each other along the Cabinet Mountains,
a land waiting to devour the good
and the bad alike . . .*

It had been that kind of a day, the big man with the
lake-blue eyes muttered under his breath. The girl
first, he added with a silent oath as he moved the
Ovaro slowly downward, the horse's jet black fore-
and hind-quarters and white midsection glistening
against the deep-green, tapering leaves of the bur oaks
that dotted the hillside. The damn girl, he swore again.
She had shattered the peace of the morning and turned
the whole day around. Now, instead of feeling rested
and refreshed, his head still throbbed and his mouth
felt as though he were chewing cotton. Skye Fargo
swore again under his breath.

His thoughts reeled backward. Not far. It had only
been a few hours before. He had taken off clothes,
down to almost nothing, and stretched his near-naked
self out on a flat, soft bed of mountain fern moss to let
the hot sun bake down on him. He had guessed it
would take the entire morning and maybe a little more
for the sun to sweat the bourbon out of him and stop
the pounding in his head. All the result of a night of

carousing in West Hollow, just east of Whitefish. His thoughts reeled back a little further, to the night with Will and Tom Brady. It had been part reunion and part celebration. He had just brought a herd to Will and Tom that blazed a new trail up from Wind River land in Wyoming, and they were all in a mood for celebrating. It had been a long, hot, and hard trek through Cheyenne and Shoshoni country, but the new trail he'd blazed was better than the old, protected and less mountainous.

It had indeed been a time for celebrating and they'd done so with a vengeance, exchanging too many stories and downing too many bourbons. They'd stayed in the dance hall in West Hollow and the girl had come to the table when the night was late. Strangely enough, he remembered her more clearly than he did much else—young, thin, pretty in a wan kind of way. He had shrugged her away at first. He was never much one for dance-hall girls.

But she had stayed, pleasantly persistent, and when Tom and Will went under, he found himself in a room with her. She was new to the dance hall, she told him. Maybe because of that, maybe because she was surprisingly tender with her own kind of quiet sweetness—small breasts, a little on the flat side, a thin body—she had worked her way into his arms.

Perhaps all the bourbon helped, but she had managed to generate her own sensuousness—surprising, given the lack of sensuousness in her body. She had brought the rest of the bottle along to keep the mood going, and managed to drink a good part of it herself. He didn't remember much about the rest of the night, except the lovemaking, and that only in a vague way.

The dawn had come when he pulled himself together and weaved his way from the room with a glance back at the slender girl asleep in the bed. When he reached the street outside, his head felt as though a buffalo stampede was taking place inside it. He climbed onto the Ovaro, rode from town, and headed into the low hills. He managed to ride for over an hour when he came to the patch of soft mountain fern moss in the hot sun and decided that Mother Nature's healing was his best hope.

Clothes shed, he had slept in the hot, baking sun, dimly aware he was perspiring profusely, for at least two hours, he guessed. Then the clatter of hoofbeats had broken the silence of the small glade. His hand was on the butt of the big Colt at his side before he pulled his eyes open, to see a horse being reined to a sharp halt. He blinked away sleep and the figure in the saddle took on shape, then details. He saw a young woman, dark-brown hair pulled back in a bun, a long neck, straight nose, snappingly bright-blue eyes, nice lips: an attractive face, though a little severely held together. She wore a white blouse, buttoned to the neck, and a modest swell of breasts pushed the front out.

"Thank God," she said. "I've been riding all over to find somebody. My wagon's broken. I need help."

Skye Fargo blinked, licked his dry lips with a tongue hardly less dry, and saw her eyes take in his near nakedness with disapproval.

"Would you put on your clothes and follow me?" she said, her tone more a command than a request.

He grimaced as a particularly sharp throb of pain went through his head. "Go away, girlie," he said, and lay back on the moss. The pain in his head lessened at once and he sighed in relief.

"What did you say?" The young woman frowned.

"Go away. Forget it," Fargo said. He was to meet Jake Carmody in Loggerville by the end of the day. Sheriff Jake Carmody. He didn't aim to do that still suffering from a hangover. He needed more peace and quiet, and he looked up at the young woman. "Keep riding, honey. You'll find somebody," he said, and closed his eyes. The throbbing lessened at once.

"I've been riding for hours in all directions. You're the first person I've come upon," he heard her say.

"Keep looking," he murmured.

"Dammit, you've got to come with me. I've valuable cargo in my wagon."

His eyes stayed closed. "Get lost."

"You are coming with me," he heard her insist, her voice rising.

"On your way, honey. You're interrupting medical treatment. I've got to rest my head," he said, his eyes staying closed.

"You mean your self-indulgent, drink-sodden body."

"Whatever. But I'm staying right here." He heard her wheel the horse, a sudden sharp movement, and he pulled his eyes open in time to see her lean from the saddle and scoop up his trousers, shirt, and boots.

"Then you won't be needing these," she flung back as she sent the horse into a gallop.

"Goddamn," Fargo swore as he jumped to his feet, ignoring the pain that shot through his head. "You come back here," he shouted, but she had already vanished into the trees. "Goddamn little bitch," Fargo swore aloud, bent over, and winced as the blood rushed through his head and brought a sharp pain with it. He picked up his gun belt, strapped it over his drawers, and started for the Ovaro, cursing as he stepped on a sharp piece of stone. He pulled himself into the saddle and started into the trees after her.

She had left riding hard and he didn't try to catch up to her, for every jounce sent a stab of pain through him. He followed the hoofprints of her horse up a slope that leveled off, rose again, and crested. He moved down the far side of the slope. He spotted the wagon in a hollow along a mountain path. An Owensboro Texas wagon outfitted with top bows and canvas, rear wheels larger than the front, which made for both good traction and good steering. Almost as much room inside as in a Conestoga, he knew, and his eyes went to the young woman. She had dismounted and waited alongside the wagon, a cool appraisal in her eyes as he rode to a halt.

"My, it seems you can stir yourself," she said tartly. "All you need is the right motivation."

Fargo stayed silent as he swung from the Ovaro, sweeping her Owensboro again with a quick glance. He took in the team of solid horses hitched to the front, and his eyes moved to the rear wheel, which jutted out at a crazy angle from the body of the wagon. It had gone into a deep hole. He swept the rear carriage of the wagon with a quick, experienced eye: the wheel appeared broken to the novice, but it wasn't. The hub was still on the axle skein and he saw that the axle itself had shifted all the way to one side when the wheel went into the hole. The play was built into the gear to allow for just such moments, all designed to prevent a wheel from snapping off against a stiff, unyielding axletree.

Some axles had a little too much play in them and could cause a wheel to come loose. This was probably one of those, but in this instance it had done its job. With the right maneuver, the axle would shift back and the wheel go into place. He paused, glanced inside the wagon, and saw only traveling bags and hatboxes. "This your valuable cargo?" he asked.

"Part of it," she said, unfazed.

He sauntered toward her and saw her eyes move across the muscled symmetry of his near-naked body. "The wheel's not broken," he told her. "Lift the rear of the wagon at the same time you set the team to pulling. Everything will slip back into place."

"You can help me do that right now," she said.

Fargo's smile was made of ice. "Go to hell, honey," he said as he moved closer to her.

"I can't do it by myself, and you're here," she said with just a trace of smugness.

He moved a step closer before his arms shot out with the speed of a rattler's strike. He curled one hand around her waist, the other around the back of her neck, and yanked her forward. She came with a half-scream of surprise and he dropped to one knee and turned her over the other. He felt the firmness of her body as he held her with one hand pressed into her back while he brought his other palm down real hard on her rear. Her first scream was a mixture of fury and pain. He administered at least a half-dozen stinging slaps to her rear, and her last two gasped screams were more pain than fury. He stood up and dumped her onto the ground and stared down at her for a moment.

"You probably should've had more of that when you were growing up," he said.

Her even lips worked for a moment before the words came. "You rotten bastard," she said as he strode away and scooped up his clothes. He turned as she regained her feet, put a hand to her rear, and drew it away at once as her lips parted in a short gasp of pain. "You are the lowest, rottenest, meanest man I've ever met," she said.

"Be glad I didn't pull your britches down," Fargo said blandly.

Her eyes were snapping darts of blue fire. "I'm surprised you didn't," she flung back tartly.

"I thought about it," he said as he walked to the Ovaro.

"What stopped you? Certainly not becoming a gentleman all of a sudden," she hissed.

"I figured you for a bony, flat ass not worth the seeing," he tossed back. She didn't see his smile as he swung onto the pinto, but he saw her casting about for something to throw as he started to ride away.

"Rotten, stinking, no-good bastard," she screamed after him.

He rode on without a glance back, his head pounding fiercely again. He needed another few hours of sweating in the sun, he realized, and he rode back to the flat bed of moss, stretched out once again, but kept his clothes closer this time. Arrogant little spitfire, he muttered to himself as he thought about the girl; maybe she'd learned a lesson about high-handed behavior. He closed his eyes and was asleep in minutes, letting his body absorb the welcome heat of the sun's burning rays.

The afternoon had begun to move toward its end when he woke, stretched, and smiled as he felt not the hint of an ache or throb. He dressed quickly and climbed onto the pinto. It was time to head to Loggerville and Sheriff Jake Carmody. As he rode, he realized he hadn't seen Jake in at least three years. Jake had been talking about retiring then, Fargo remembered. Jake Carmody had to be in his mid-fifties, a good, honest man, not too hard yet not intimidated, the perfect sheriff for a town such as Loggerville.

The town nestled at the foot of the Cabinet Mountains, one of the many individual mountain ranges that made up the giant sweep of the Rockies. Loggerville had more than the usual share of tough, rough loggers and mountain men, some mean at heart but most only mean by liquor. Yet there were plenty of men on the run who stopped at a town such as Loggerville while they decided whether to dare the wild fastness of the mountains or turn and flee in another direction.

Fargo turned the Ovaro along the hillside where he had pursued the young woman. It was on his way north and he reached the hollow and the path to find the wagon gone. Someone had come along and helped her, or she'd gone out and found someone else. Either way she had managed, and he wasn't surprised at that. Not with her talent of concocting a story about valuable cargo and her spitfire determination. Now that he'd rid himself of his stupendous hangover and his own anger had died down, he found himself curious about her. What was an attractive young woman doing in these wild foothills all alone in a big Texas mountain wagon, he wondered. She was quick-minded as well as quick-tempered. He'd learned that in the few brief moments he'd been with her. And one thing more . . . He smiled. Her ass hadn't been at all flat and boney under his hand. But he pushed further thoughts about her from his mind. He had to get to Loggerville and Jake Carmody.

That had been his day, and his thoughts had come full circle. And now this, Fargo swore as he threaded his way down the hillside. The figure lay facedown at the bottom of the slope, hat still on. Fargo swore again under his breath. Only one man that he knew of wore that hat, an extra-large-brimmed, white stetson with a tan band. Jake Carmody. Fargo's eyes swept the bur oaks that spread along both sides of the bottom of the slope, but he saw nothing move. He spurred the pinto into a trot and reached the bottom of the hill, where he landed on the balls of his feet before the horse came to a halt.

He dropped to one knee beside Jake's burly figure. The sheriff was alive, Fargo quickly saw with relief, his breathing steady. He turned the man over and saw the bloody gash along the side of his temple. He pushed the wide-brimmed stetson from Jake's head, took a kerchief and water from his canteen, and applied the cold compress to the wound. He had repeated the compress four times when he saw the sheriff's eyes slowly come open, stare up at him, and finally the blankness in them filled with recognition.

"Jesus, Fargo. How'd you get here?" Jake Carmody asked.

"Just what I was going to ask you," Fargo said.

The older man pushed himself up on one elbow and winced at the pain. "Old age, that's how, goddammit," Jake Carmody said. He paused and took in Fargo's questioning frown. "I was bringing two prisoners back when they jumped me," Jake explained. "One of them made a funny motion and I pulled my gun on him and the other one hit me from the back. My own damn fault. I let them sucker me into it. Even so, ten years ago I'd have been quick enough to avoid it. Maybe even five years ago. But not now." The older man started to rise and fell back in pain. "Jesus, guess I twisted my leg when I fell," he said.

"Stay right here. Rest yourself. I'll get them back for you," Fargo said.

Jake Carmody's eyes lighted with gratitude. "Would you, old friend?" he said. "I sure as hell can't do it. They took my gun and horse with them. Two weasely range rats wanted for murderin' an old trapper and stealin' his pelts. The tall one's Bud Royce, the short one's Enoch Cable."

"Stay right here. Lie back and rest. Keep the cold compress against your head," Fargo said as he rose and swung onto the Ovaro.

"Watch yourself, Fargo. They're not going to take to coming back with you," the sheriff said.

"That'll be their choice," Fargo said grimly, and moved the pinto in a slow circle until he spotted the hoofprints, three horses moving north. With a wave back at Jake, he rode on and followed the fresh prints with ease.

They had raced away, hoofmarks dug deep into the soil, but then slowed, Fargo noted. They stayed at a leisurely pace, plainly confident Jake wouldn't be following after them. The prints swung into a forest of red ash and emerged to move down to a narrow path along a low plateau dotted with box elder. Fargo stayed on the low hill and finally spotted them as they rode side by side, with Jake's horse following behind. Though both wore gun belts, they had only one gun, Jake's, and Fargo saw it on the hip of the tall figure. Bud Royce, Jake had called him, and he sat a full head taller than his companion.

Fargo moved the pinto slowly along the top of the low hill, through a line of young cottonwoods. He stayed there as he passed the two riders below. He wanted to avoid coming up behind them—a precipitate chase, which could lose at least one on him. When he was some two hundred yards beyond the duo, he turned the pinto downward and was casually riding along the path when the two men caught up to him. He half-turned in the saddle as the two riders came closer, allowed a friendly smile that took in both men.

" 'Afternoon, gents," he said, and saw both men regard him with the kind of expression a fox views a chicken.

He let them draw to a halt, and when he turned back again, the big Colt was in his hand. "Drop the gun, Bud," he growled, and the tall man's eyes widened in surprise. "Nice and slow," he added. Royce stared at him as he slowly lifted the gun from the holster and let it drop to the ground.

"Who the hell are you, mister?" Bud Royce growled.

"Sheriff Carmody sent me," Fargo said. Both men shot glances of astonishment at each other. "He was sorry you left without even saying good-bye. Bad manners. You'll have to come back and stay after school. Get off your horses. You first, Royce." The man slid from the saddle under Fargo's gaze. "You next," Fargo ordered the shorter figure.

"You're smarter than the old man," Royce muttered.

"Step back, away from the horses," Fargo said, and both men obeyed. He waited till they were back far enough to lower the Colt for a moment as he leaned forward and took hold of the reins of both horses, backed the pinto, and tied the reins to the saddle horn of Jake's horse.

"You boys are going to walk back," he said. "It'll take all the extra energy out of you." He half-turned to pull the horses facing the same direction when he caught the faint sound; fabric being brushed aside. He whirled just in time to see the shorter one yank the gun out from inside his shirt. He flung himself sideways from the saddle as Enoch Cable fired, but he felt the sharp, searing pain along the top of his forehead.

He hit the ground on his back as he shook away a wave of fog that tried to settle over him; he managed to roll and heard another shot slam into the ground inches from his head. The fog tried to descend on him again, but he shook his head and it lifted in time for him to see the short figure rushing at him, the gun upraised. He managed to kick out, the blow landing squarely in Cable's groin and the man doubled up in a curse of pain. Fargo rolled, brought his gun hand up to fire, and with a curse realized that his hand was empty. The Colt had fallen from his grip when he hit the ground; he spied it in the grass a dozen feet away. He also saw the tall figure racing to pounce on it and he flung himself forward. He reached the gun just as Bud Royce did, and closed one hand around the man's wrist. He yanked, but Royce kept his grip on the butt of the pistol and Fargo rolled sideways and took the tall figure with him.

Out of the corner of his eye he glimpsed Enoch Cable, one hand still holding his groin, start to pull himself to his feet. Royce tried to wrestle his wrist free, but Fargo's grip was viselike and he arched his back, rolled again, and took Bud with him. This time he twisted hard on Royce's wrist and the man swore in pain as the Colt fell from his fingers. Fargo released his grip and scooped up the revolver as Royce wrestled himself free. The man half-rolled, half-dived along the ground, but Fargo's eyes were on Cable, who came toward him with the gun in his hand. The Trailsman fired two shots from the Colt, his arm resting on the ground, and the short figure shuddered, staggered sideways, and collapsed.

Fargo spun to see Royce scooping up Jake Carmody's gun. He fired the Colt as Royce whirled on him and the man's tall body straightened out as he flew backward, a small fountain of red spurting from his chest. He hit the ground and lay still, and Fargo rose to his feet, holstered the Colt, and moved from the short figure to the tall one as he picked up both guns. He stared at the gun Cable had pulled from inside his shirt. If he'd had it all along, why hadn't he pulled it on the sheriff. And if he didn't have it, then where did he get it?

Tabling the questions, Fargo lifted each man face-down across his horse and climbed onto the Ovaro to lead the silent procession back the way he'd come.

Dusk had begun to settle over the hills when he reached the spot where Jake Carmody waited, sprawled atop a flat rock.

The sheriff slowly pushed to his feet as the slow line came into sight and he cast a grim glance at the lifeless forms draped across their saddles. "Decided to give you trouble, did they?" he grunted.

"The short one came up with another gun," Fargo said, and saw the expression of horror slide across Jake's face.

"Oh, God, Jesus, I'm sorry, Fargo. My old Remington forty-four. It was in my saddlebag."

"They must've looked inside and found it," Fargo said.

"Dammit, old friend, this is just one more reason I'm packing it in. Reflexes are gone, eye's gone, and the memory's going along with everything else," Jake Carmody said. "Let's get to town. We've a lot to talk about."

# BLAZING NEW TRAILS
# WITH SKYE FARGO

☐ **THE TRAILSMAN #106: SIERRA SHOOT-OUT by Jon Sharpe.** Skye Fargo found anglo ranchers and Mexican settlers, embattled missionaries and marauding banditos, all waging a war where he couldn't tell good guys from bad without a gun. (167465—$3.50)

☐ **THE TRAILSMAN #107: GUNSMOKE GULCH by Jon Sharpe.** Skye Fargo blasts a white-slaving ring apart and discovers that a beauty named Annie has a clue to a gold mine worth slaying for—a proposition that makes Skye ready to blaze a trail through a gunsmoke screen of lethal lies. (168038—$3.50)

☐ **THE TRAILSMAN #108: PAWNEE BARGAIN by Jon Sharpe.** Skye Fargo is caught in a cross fire between military madness and Indian barbarity. (168577—$3.50)

☐ **THE TRAILSMAN #109: LONE STAR LIGHTNING by Jon Sharpe.** Skye Fargo on a Texas manhunt with two deadly weapons—a blazing gun and a fiery female. (168801—$3.50)

☐ **THE TRAILSMAN #110: COUNTERFEIT CARGO by Jon Sharpe.** The pay was too good for Skye Fargo to turn down, so he's guiding a wagon train loaded with evil and heading for hell. (168941—$3.50)